East Side Blvd.
Muskogee, OK
682-4249

She turned around to find Justin looking down at her.

"Why don't you go change?" he said in an uncharacteristically tender voice. "You must be exhausted."

The display of consideration from this ice man brought a smile to Philadelphia's lips. "As a matter of fact, I am. Are you being nice, Starbuck?"

He wasn't sure if she was teasing or being sarcastic. With her, he wasn't sure about a damn thing. Except that her smile was getting to him.

"Yes."

"Oh...I thought maybe you were afraid that I'd steal your aunt's gold fillings after she fell asleep."

"Do you enjoy being irritating?"

"I don't know." Her smile flashed. "Let me explore it a little more."

Suddenly, it was too much: the light scent tickling his senses, the teasing mouth curved up toward him, the demands that ran through his own body. "Then explore this while you're at it."

He had no idea why he kissed her. No idea that he was *going* to...until he did.

Dear Reader,

Welcome to Silhouette Romance—experience the magic of the wonderful world where two people fall in love. Meet heroines who will make you cheer for their happiness, and heroes (be they the boy next door or a handsome, mysterious stranger) who will win your heart. Silhouette Romance reflects the magic of love—sweeping you away with books that will make you laugh and cry; heartwarming, poignant stories that will move you time and time again.

In the next few months, we're publishing romances by many of your all-time favorites such as Diana Palmer, Brittany Young, Annette Broadrick and many others. Your response to these authors and others in Silhouette Romance has served as a touchstone for us, and we're pleased to bring you more books with Silhouette's distinctive medley of charm, wit and—above all—*romance*.

During 1991, we have many special events planned. Don't miss our WRITTEN IN THE STARS series. Each month in 1991, we're proud to present you with a book that focuses on the hero—and his astrological sign.

I hope you'll enjoy this book and all of the stories to come. Come home to romance—Silhouette Romance—for always!

Sincerely,

Tara Gavin
Senior Editor

MARIE FERRARELLA

The Undoing of Justin Starbuck

Silhouette Romance

Published by Silhouette Books New York

America's Publisher of Contemporary Romance

To Dottie Snyder and Kathy Corbett
for listening

SILHOUETTE BOOKS
300 E. 42nd St., New York, N.Y. 10017

THE UNDOING OF JUSTIN STARBUCK

Copyright © 1991 by Marie Rydzynski-Ferrarella

MORE ABOUT THE CAPRICORN MAN.
Copyright © 1991 by Harlequin Enterprises B.V.

The publisher acknowledges Lydia Lee's contribution to
the afterword contained in this book.

All rights reserved. Except for use in any review,
the reproduction or utilization of this work in
whole or in part in any form by any electronic,
mechanical or other means, now known or
hereafter invented, including xerography,
photocopying and recording, or in any information
storage or retrieval system, is forbidden without
the permission of Silhouette Books, 300 E. 42nd St.,
New York, N.Y. 10017

ISBN: 0-373-08766-7

First Silhouette Books printing January 1991

All the characters in this book are fictitious. Any
resemblance to actual persons, living or dead, is
purely coincidental.

®: Trademark used under license and
registered in the United States Patent and
Trademark Office and in other countries.

Printed in the U.S.A.

MARIE FERRARELLA

was born in Europe, raised in New York City and now lives in Southern California. She describes herself as the tired mother of two over-energetic children and the contented wife of one wonderful man. She is thrilled to be following her dream of writing fulltime.

A Note from the Author

Dear Reader,

I was very pleased and honored to be asked to write the lead book for Silhouette's new WRITTEN IN THE STARS series. Pleased, honored and nervous. Quickly, I rushed to my bookstore to read everything I could about the stars. I was richly rewarded.

Research taught me a few very interesting things. First and foremost, I now finally have an excuse for being the way I am. When someone, such as my husband, complains about the fact that I do everything at ninety miles an hour (well, except for one thing—I park the car slowly) I can now in all good conscience point out the fact that I'm an Aries. If I drive people crazy by always being early, compulsive and talking faster than the speed of sound, it's not my fault. I am just a product of various astrological happenings. (I have to blame something.)

I also found out that my husband, a Taurus, and I are the least likely signs in the Zodiac to have a successful marriage. I'm not sure how many years there are in a successful marriage, but we're up to seventeen now.

Seriously though, it was a lot of fun delving into personality traits attributed to various positions of the stars and then utilizing this information when creating my characters and their particular romance story. It gave me a whole new set of circumstances and a new perspective to consider. I hope you have as much fun reading this book as I had writing it. Once again, thank you for being there. I couldn't make it without you.

Sincerely,
Marie Ferrarella

Prologue

"What's your sign, girl?"

Philadelphia Jones had expected any one of a number of questions to be directed her way after having been shown into the opulently decorated living room and coming face-to-face with Rosalind Starbuck. This was not one of them.

She stared at the older woman. Rosalind sat back on a piece of futuristic furniture that was comprised of a multitude of colorful pillows surrounding her like a protective cocoon. The pillows, in various sizes and shapes, were arranged so that when she leaned from side to side, Rosalind did not put any undue strain on her back. A gold cane with a jeweled head rested against one leg of the chair, catching the afternoon light.

Philadelphia did her best to match the aura of self-confidence that Rosalind exuded. She really needed this job and was determined to make the most of the interview. This position was what she wanted, what she needed. It had been her advertisement in the "Positions Wanted" column of

New World Magazine that had gotten her here in the first place. The ad had been born of desperation, an emotion she was not unacquainted with, but one that she had no taste for. Philadelphia remembered the carefully-worded phrases now as if it were right in front of her eyes.

Energetic twenty-five-year-old female seeks position with elderly woman as live-in companion. Willing to work hard. Has two-year-old son.

She had been relieved and grateful when Rosalind's housekeeper had called her yesterday afternoon to arrange an interview. Philadelphia had looked forward to the interview and to the job she already felt she had. That was the way she did things, projecting herself in the most positive manner she could. Mark had almost made her forget the cardinal rule that had seen her through so much. But Mark was gone.

She mustered a smile now at the woman who had been a living legend, known as much for her temper as her beauty. "Excuse me?"

Rosalind frowned, the furrows deep in her once-famous face. "Your sign, girl. What sign were you born under?" Rosalind sighed audibly when Philadelphia failed to respond immediately. "Your astrological sign. Don't tell me that you don't know your sign."

Philadelphia had no idea what her sign was. Though her interests were eclectic, astrology had never been among them. She hoped that wouldn't cost her the position, but she could no more lie than she could cheat or steal. Or fly. "I don't know. Is it important?"

Rosalind shifted in her seat and grimaced, more from pain than impatience. "Of course it's important. How else am I to know if you'll drive me crazy or be so obstinate that we won't get along?''

Philadelphia had strong suspicions that things might be the other way around, but kept the thought, and her grin, to herself.

Rosalind tapped her right foot. A pale pink bedroom slipper peeked out from beneath a billowing rose raw-silk caftan. The other foot, Philadelphia noted, remained still and was set at an awkward angle. That was probably the one that made the cane necessary.

"Well, when is your birthday?"

Philadelphia returned her gaze to the woman's carefully made up face. "The end of March."

"That makes you an Aries."

"Does it?"

She tried to sound as if she were truly interested. She wished she could sit down. But Rosalind seemed quite content in carrying on the interview in the manner of a queen interviewing a lady-in-waiting. She sat and the interviewee stood until otherwise instructed. Philadelphia remembered that Rosalind had once played Queen Elizabeth I on the screen. Apparently some roles were hard to give up.

Philadelphia wondered if Rosalind Starbuck was really as tough as they said or if, as with all legends, the facts were exaggerated. She had a feeling that in this particular case, the truth was not that far from the legend.

Rosalind considered Philadelphia for a bare moment. "Aries. That means you're stubborn."

"I don't—"

A wide hand, diamond encrusted rings on each finger except for the thumb, waved words into dismissal. "Now, don't try to deny it. I know my stars."

If you're thinking of intimidating me, I've stood up to far worse than you, Philadelphia thought, amused. "I'm sure you do, and I wasn't about to deny anything. I was going to say I don't let my personal traits get in the way of my job."

Rosalind acknowledged the statement with the smallest of nods. "Admirable."

Philadelphia watched the older woman's expression. "I think so."

Rosalind cocked an eyebrow as she leveled a steady gaze at Philadelphia. "You have spunk, girl. I admire spunk. Had some myself when I was young."

This time, Philadelphia did grin. "I don't think you lost any along the way."

Perfect dark eyebrows gathered close like storm clouds above startling violet eyes. "You're impertinent."

There was no use denying the obvious. "Yes, ma'am."

Rosalind allowed herself a smile that took in all three of her well-pampered chins. "Good for you."

Philadelphia let go of the sigh of relief she was holding back. It was beginning to look as though she would get this job, as if things were going to be all right, after all. At least for a little while. Which was all she had ever asked for.

"Thank you."

"Don't be so hasty to thank me." Rosalind looked down at the magazine she had opened next to her on the chair. She jabbed at the box she had circled. She did it for form's sake. Without her glasses, which she never wore when she first met people, she couldn't see the words, but there was no need. She had memorized them. Some things were second nature to her. "It says here you have a son."

"Yes."

Rosalind raised her head and gave the young blonde before her a piercing look. "Noisy?"

Philadelphia thought another word might do in this instance. "Normal."

Rosalind leaned back slightly in her chair, resting her bare arms on the gold brocade sides. "It's been a long time since there's been a child in this house."

Rosalind Starbuck was silent for a moment. If there was anything the former star knew how to do, Philadelphia guessed, it was pause dramatically. Philadelphia recalled the last Rosalind Starbuck movie she had seen on a late-night telecast. She had been Rosalind Roman when the movie was made, a hundred pounds lighter and fifty years younger. Her hair had been naturally black then rather than the result of dyes carefully applied by a French hairdresser. But the zest she exuded was something that hadn't changed. It was said that in her youth, she could cow powerful heads of studios. Philadelphia didn't doubt it. She found the prospect of working for the woman exciting, an unexpected bonus to balance out the dilemma she found herself in.

But if Rosalind had an aversion to children, then all bets were off. "Will that be a problem?" Once again, Philadelphia found herself holding her breath.

"That remains to be seen, doesn't it?"

Philadelphia took that as a plus. Hope seemed to appear on the horizon.

"My nephew Justin taught me to be thorough." She allowed a smile to curve her mouth. "Justin is the practical type, but that's par for a Capricorn. Do you have any references?"

"As a companion? No, I've never done this sort of thing before," Philadelphia admitted truthfully.

Rosalind's growing smile told Philadelphia that the woman appreciated not being lied to. "That makes us even. I've never had a companion before." The smile spread, turning into a wide, meaningful one that lit up her face. There was a wicked gleam in her eyes. She was almost beautiful again. "Not a female one at any rate."

Philadelphia knew about the consorts, the lovers Rosalind had been said to have after the much-older Alfred Starbuck had died, leaving her a very wealthy, very lusty widow at the age of forty-eight. Ever since the call from Rosalind's estate had come, Philadelphia had read everything she could get her hands on about the former movie star.

Rosalind's expression changed to a thoughtful one, and Philadelphia knew she was being sized up.

"Tell me." Her words were spoken slowly, as if each was measured. "Why does a young girl want to tie herself down to being a companion to an elderly lady like me?"

The obvious response was to murmur words that would flatter, saying something about Rosalind not being at all elderly. She certainly wasn't doddering, but at an admitted seventy-two—and there were rumors she was older—Rosalind couldn't be described as a spritely young thing, either. Feeling more comfortable with honesty, Philadelphia answered simply, "I need a position that'll let me spend more time with my little boy."

The sun shone in through the filmy curtains at Rosalind's back, bathing her in an almost ethereal light. "What was your last position?"

"I was a computer programmer for a company that went bankrupt. I hardly ever saw Ricky awake."

"Ricky?" Rosalind rolled the name around on her tongue, as if doing so would give her further insight. "That's your son, I take it, and not your lazy husband."

"I don't have a husband, lazy or otherwise. Eric, I call him Ricky," she explained, "is my son."

Philadelphia braced herself for more questions or possibly censure. She hadn't admitted outright that she hadn't been married to Ricky's father, but that could be inferred from her statement. She did not intend to lie about the situation if asked.

Just as the silence became uncomfortable, Rosalind rose majestically to her feet. It didn't matter that she barely topped five feet when she stood. The aura she projected was at least a foot taller. "When can you start?"

Philadelphia saw no reason to hide her surprise this time. "No more questions?"

Rosalind leaned heavily on her cane as she moved away from the chair. "Oh, there'll be questions . . . Philadelphia, is it?" She looked over her shoulder to see Philadelphia nod. "Such as where your parents got such a ridiculous name?"

She had heard that one before. As a child, she had hated her name. Now, she rather liked its unique sound. "I was born in a Greyhound bus station in Philadelphia."

"Interesting. Anyway, as I was saying, there'll be lots of questions. I'll ask them as I think of them. Right now, I see no reason not to hire you." Rosalind turned slowly to face her. Arthritis had made her body far less responsive than she liked. "I go by instinct."

"And the stars."

Rosalind grinned broadly. "You catch on fast, Philadelphia."

"I try."

Rosalind laughed, pleased. "We'll get on, girl." She leaned forward slightly, one hand pressing hard on the cane. The other was extended toward Philadelphia. The afternoon light fractured into a rainbow after passing through the diamond engagement ring.

Philadelphia slipped her hand into the bejeweled one. The handshake was firm and binding. Neither woman had any doubt of that.

Chapter One

"Justin, there's a call for you on line two," Sherwood Simpson said as he looked into Justin Starbuck's office. He jerked a thumb toward the reception area. "From the sound of it, Frieda seems to think that the woman is a bit upset."

Upset. That seemed to be the operative word around the Foundation. After six years, Justin was getting used to it. Poverty was definitely an upsetting prospect. But if he talked to each supplicating person who called the Foundation directly, the telephone receiver might as well be permanently attached to his head.

"Woody, you know I don't take these calls. That's Walker's area—"

"Frieda said that the woman told her she was down to her last dime and she demands to speak to you personally. She doesn't want to talk to Walker. She's called twice in the last ten minutes." Woody looked down at his Rolex. "Considering that it's only 9:18, I'd say she was rather desperate."

Justin let out a sigh and massaged the bridge of his nose. A little after nine and he felt drained. He needed a vacation, except that there was nowhere he really felt like going. Maybe he'd spend an extended weekend at Roz's. He hadn't been there in a long time. Too long. He began to smile, just anticipating it. If he found a spare minute after the meeting, he'd place a call to her and ask if she was free.

Dropping his hand, he looked at the flashing red light on his telephone. He supposed that there'd be no harm in answering the call himself. The board meeting wouldn't be for at least another forty minutes. He thought of the things he had to do before catching the plane for Fresno tonight at six; five minutes wouldn't put a crimp in his schedule one way or another. Maybe it wouldn't hurt to be in touch once in a while with the people whose problems he was attempting to solve.

"Tell Frieda I'll take it." He jabbed at the urgently blinking light as Woody slipped out of the room. "Justin Starbuck."

"Finally."

For a supplicating person, she was awfully arrogant, he thought. He had made it his life's work to help the poor. That didn't mean he had to like them, or people in general for that matter. Still, there were responsibilities. He believed in a fair balance. And poverty was a word he had always hated. "I'm sure that Ms. Reynolds informed you of our policy."

Yes, Ms. Reynolds had jabbered at her for a full three minutes about how *terribly* busy Mr. Justin Starbuck was until Philadelphia had shouted that she demanded to speak to him in person, busy schedule be damned. He was going to want to take this call, she had assured the officious secretary. She hadn't been given the chance to explain anything or even to mention Rosalind's name. The secretary had talked much too fast for that. It was Philadelphia's tone that managed to convey the urgency of the situation. She had gotten Justin's number by making a call to Angie at the house, then had used up all her spare change calling this man who wouldn't answer his phone. Down to the last two dimes in her jeans, she wasn't about to be put off again.

"Mr. Starbuck, if you people would let me get a word in edgewise, I could tell you that this doesn't have anything to do with your policy. This is about—"

Justin decided he should hang up. Everybody always thought their case was unique and that the rules didn't apply. There had been more than a spate of nut calls since the Foundation had opened its doors. But the woman's low, whiskey voice, full of frustration, somehow intrigued him. Maybe he needed that vacation more than he realized. "Just who are you?"

Philadelphia fumed. Again she had been interrupted. Why wasn't anyone letting her finish her sentence? she thought in irritated exasperation. Maybe he was one of those snobs that wouldn't speak to someone without a proper introduction. Philadelphia blew at her bangs with an annoyed breath. "Philadelphia Jones."

He tried to picture a face that would go along with the name and came up empty. But the whiskey-edged voice had him trying. "Well, Ms. Jones..."

She thought she detected condescension and wondered why on earth Rosalind had implored her to call this man to her bedside. How in heaven's name could someone so pompous sounding be related to that wonderful woman in the first place? Then Philadelphia remembered that it was by marriage rather than by blood. That explained a lot.

"Mr. Starbuck," she shouted to cut through his endless rhetoric. Three people stared at her as they passed through the hall. With effort, Philadelphia lowered her voice but didn't unclench her teeth. "I am calling about your aunt."

He stopped dead. "My aunt?" He thought of Rosalind immediately.

Maybe he had more than one, Philadelphia thought suddenly. "Rosalind Starbuck."

Justin's hand tightened on the receiver. Fear filled his mind. Not Aunt Roz. She was too full of life. Too—

Slowly, he forced himself to stay in control. He was jumping to conclusions. This was probably just some message she was having relayed. Instinct, born of pessimism, told him he was wrong. "What about my aunt?"

Philadelphia heard the difference in his tone. There was no longer that icy remoteness evident. "She asked me to call you—"

"Why? Why can't she call herself?"

God, she was tired. She dragged her hand through her hair and closed her eyes, realizing that she hadn't really sat down since she had leapt out of bed that morning

"Because she's hooked up to monitors and can't reach the phone, that's why."

There, that got him. Philadelphia felt a certain amount of satisfaction at having utterly silenced the exasperating man on the other end of the line.

Justin gripped the receiver more tightly. A line of perspiration formed along his spine and temples. He refused to acknowledge it or the very real fear that was licking at him. There had to be some mistake. "What are you talking about? Where is she?"

"St. Mary's Hospital. The doctor is pretty sure she's had a heart attack. She's asking for you. Hello? Mr. Starbuck, are you there?" A dial tone answered her question. "Terrific."

Philadelphia sighed and hung up the phone in the lobby, then ran her hand through her hair again. She still hadn't had a chance to comb it. Or to put on any makeup. She had been too worried.

A nurse and orderly pushing a gurney rushed by. Philadelphia sidestepped them without really seeing either one.

Because there was nothing else to do, she wandered back to the sofa in the waiting area on the fifth floor and picked up the cardboard cup she had left. The coffee was cold and tasted terrible. It didn't matter. It had tasted terrible when it had first come out of the machine. It was the caffeine she was after. Although her nerves were on edge, she needed something to keep her going until she got a chance to corner the doctor and find out how Rosalind was doing.

It wasn't a shock to realize that after only two weeks, she really loved that old lady. Philadelphia had never played coy with her feelings or kept them locked up for that matter. That was part of her problem.

Part of her sign, Rosalind had told her.

Two weeks. It had seemed much longer than that. In two weeks, she had become entrenched, taken up a routine and felt a part of something. Rosalind, with her boisterous, bombastic ways, had made Philadelphia feel as if she had finally come home. It had been a long time since she had felt like that. Not since the year her parents died, just when she had gone off to college. She hadn't even felt like that when she had lived with Mark. She had been restless then. She wasn't any longer.

Philadelphia stretched out her legs before her. There was a stack of well-thumbed magazines on the table to her left. They held no interest. The only things that did were the automatic doors just down the hall. The doors that led into the coronary-care unit. She wanted someone wearing a white coat to come out and tell her that everything was going to be all right.

She waited and she watched.

The housekeeper's scream had awakened her at five. Each morning, Angie brought juice and toast to Rosalind's bedroom. Philadelphia had been up early enough to witness the ritual several times. Each time Angie had passed her in the hall, grumbling audibly to herself, and Philadelphia had no doubts that Angie had grumbled every morning for the last twenty-seven years.

This morning, the grumbling had stopped abruptly, a scream taking its place. Philadelphia, trying to take advantage of the fact that Ricky was sleeping late for a change, was still in bed. She had leapt up and was at Rosalind's door in a matter of seconds, her heart pounding. She found Angie clutching Rosalind's hand, talking to her, shaking her. Rosalind hadn't responded.

The wizened old woman had looked at Philadelphia with eyes filled with fear. Philadelphia had been quick to act.

"Call 911," Philadelphia instructed. Whatever was wrong with Rosalind, she wasn't about to take chances. If she were overreacting, she'd face up to the consequences later. At that moment, all that mattered was making sure that Rosalind was all right.

The paramedics arrived within minutes of the call. Easing Philadelphia aside, they quickly confirmed her worst suspicions. From all appearances, Rosalind had suffered a heart attack.

As they lifted her onto a stretcher, Rosalind regained consciousness and murmured something about it being nice to have young men at her feet again, then fainted. Philadelphia threw on the first things she saw in her closet—ripped jeans, moccasins and an oversize sweatshirt—instructed

Angie to look after Ricky and climbed into the ambulance after the stretcher.

Rosalind opened her eyes as the doors slammed shut. "What's all the fuss?" she whispered weakly.

The ambulance lunged forward as its siren pierced the early-morning air. Philadelphia threaded her fingers through Rosalind's. The old woman's hand was clammy. Philadelphia prayed, but kept a smile fixed on her face. "You've had a heart attack."

"Nonsense." Rosalind tried to raise her hand for added emphasis but couldn't. "My heart wouldn't dare."

Don't give up, Rosalind. Hang on. "It would and it did. Apparently, it's not afraid of you like everyone else."

"Are *you* afraid of me?"

Philadelphia managed a grin. "Nope."

"Good. I hate cowards." Rosalind's voice was raspy. Her very breath rattled in her chest as it sought release. For a single moment, Philadelphia thought she saw fear flash in the older woman's eyes. And then it was gone. "Stay with me, Philadelphia."

Philadelphia blinked back tears, squeezing Rosalind's hand again. "I'm not going anywhere." It was a promise.

"Knew I was right in hiring an Aries."

"Whatever you say."

A weak smile played on the woman's pale lips. "And don't you forget it." Rosalind's unfocused eyes fluttered shut as she lapsed into unconsciousness again.

The answer was a good one. It gave Philadelphia hope. Things were going to be all right.

They *had* to be.

Chapter Two

"Justin, where are you going?" Woody cried as Justin walked quickly past him in the corridor on his way toward the front door. Woody pointed behind him. "The conference room is back there. Did you forget about the meeting?"

Damn, he *had* forgotten all about that. As soon as that woman had told him about Rosalind, he had forgotten about everything else. The meeting, so important only a few minutes ago, seemed inconsequential now. Everything was inconsequential except for his aunt's recovery.

He doubled back until he stood facing his assistant. Already a worried frown was puckering Woody's face. "I can't attend the meeting, Woody."

Woody's small, black-marble eyes bulged, making him resemble a frog in a Brooks Brothers suit. "Can't attend?" Justin had always attended all the meetings. It was unheard of to hold a meeting without him. "But—"

Every minute Justin spent explaining was one minute lost, one minute that might mean the difference between . . .

Justin took a deep breath. He put his hand on Woody's rail-thin shoulder. "Look, Woody, something's just come up and I have to leave." Justin knew that he would get more understanding and less opposition if he told Woody that his aunt had had a heart attack, but Justin didn't share his life with anyone. His private life had always been just that, private.

"You make it sound like a matter of life and death."

"No, just a matter of life." Justin refused to acknowledge the other word.

Woody had been one of the first people Justin had hired. The two men had worked together for over six years. In that time, never once had Justin missed a meeting or lost his composure. Justin was always cool under fire, reserved. He heard, he sympathized, but he didn't get close. That was a given. Woody stared at him in disbelief, as if he couldn't understand what was happening. Justin would never leave the office for personal reasons. "Is there anything I can do?"

Justin realized that he must have looked like a man possessed. For a second, he wanted to stop and thank Woody for his concern. But there was no time. Besides, he wasn't certain he knew the words for that kind of thing. Sentiment always made him feel awkward.

"No, just handle the meeting for me." He was already leaving as he made his request.

"Consider it done," Woody called after Justin's departing figure. Justin didn't hear.

Locating his navy-blue sedan, Justin got in quickly and sped out of the parking lot. He had a vague idea where St. Mary's Hospital was. His aunt had taken him there once when he was twelve and had fallen out of a tree. The fall had netted him a broken arm. She could have sent one of the servants with him, or Mallory, the chauffeur. But she had not even entertained the idea of entrusting him to someone else.

With a grin, he remembered that she took over the entire emergency room like a commando, demanding that a physician tend to her injured nephew immediately. One had, too. Justin never knew if it was because his aunt had made so much noise, or if it was because she had impressed everyone with who she was. Probably it had been a combination. He couldn't remember a single instance when Rosalind had been ignored. She had always been larger than life.

Is larger than life, he corrected himself. *Is*.

His hands felt damp on the leather-bound steering wheel as he zigged and zagged, maneuvering through heavy morning traffic as he made his way to the freeway.

A heart attack. The whole idea was too incredible to comprehend. Someone else, sure, but not her.

Rosalind was the one stable factor in his life. He couldn't conceive of life without her in it. He had been a sad, withdrawn little boy whom no one wanted around. A classic example of the poor little rich boy, he imagined. It was too far in the past for him to feel the sting of bitterness any longer. But even twenty-two years was not so long ago that he could not remember. It was Aunt Roz who had taken him to task for feeling sorry for himself then, Aunt Roz who taught him how to play poker, how to roll with punches and go on. How to hold his liquor, he thought with a grin. He had always thought of her as someone who would go on forever. Immortal.

Immortals didn't have heart attacks.

That woman with the whiskey voice had to be mistaken. For all he knew, this was some hoax. Had he been thinking clearly, he would have called the hospital before he left. Part of him thought of turning off the freeway now and finding a public phone in order to check out her story. But he was unwilling to waste even a few moments—just in case.

He realized that he was doing fifteen miles over the speed limit and glanced in his rearview mirror to see if there were any police cars following. He eased his foot on the gas pedal, though it cost him, until the speedometer read fifty-five. It'd be just his luck to be stopped and get a ticket now, of all times. He always prided himself on his control.

But the phone call had thrown him for a loop. Maybe it *was* a hoax. He'd get there and find that there was no Rosalind Starbuck in the hospital.

For once, he hoped that he was on the receiving end of a cruel joke.

She looked fragile. Oh, God, she had never looked like this, not in all the years he had known her, not even when Uncle Alfred had died.

Justin ran his hand through his sandy hair, trailing his fingers down his neck and rubbing it nervously. He'd never seen her looking so pale, so lifeless. So destructible. Tubes ran up and down her body, hooking her up to strange machines. Monitors surrounded her like alien beings.

Justin had confirmed her admission to the hospital at the front desk. The round-eyed information clerk had smiled broadly at him and told him in a pronounced Southern accent that "Miz Starbuck" was in the C.C.U. of the fifth floor. He had hurried to the bank of elevators in the rear without hearing what else she said.

Reaching the fifth floor, he realized what else the clerk had tried to tell him. No one could visit the coronary care unit without permission. A notice to that effect was posted right above a desk that barred admission to the area. But the chair behind the desk was vacant, and he was in no mood to stand around and wait. He pushed open the double doors behind the desk and looked from cubicle to curtained cubicle until he found her.

"Aunt Roz?" he said softly.

The woman didn't respond. She didn't even stir beneath all those tubes.

Fighting despair, a sensation that had eluded him since the day he had first met her, he gently curled his hand around her limp fingers and just held on tightly.

"C'mon, old girl, you can't desert me now. We've still got things to do, people to intimidate." He nearly choked out the last word. How often had he heard her laugh and say that people were easily frightened and all she wanted was to meet a handful of brave souls on this earth. "You can't just slip away like this. You're supposed to make a grand exit, remember? The way you always did in your movies."

The sound of his voice didn't rouse her the way he hoped it might. "Oh, God, Aunt Roz, why—?"

"Sir, I'm afraid you have to leave. Sir, do you hear me?"

He turned slowly, taking the opportunity to pull himself together. The face he showed to the young nurse was one that was in total control. There wasn't the slightest hint of the emotional turmoil that was bubbling just under the surface. "That's my aunt strapped to those things."

A compassionate smile creased the nurse's lips. "I'm very sorry, but hospital rules state that family members can only stay at a C.C.U. patient's bedside for five minutes every hour, and Miss Jones has already used up the allotted time." She stood to his left, her body language urging him toward the double doors through which he had entered.

Justin stared at her, not comprehending. "Miss Jones?"

"Yes. Miss Jones." The nurse repeated the name with emphasis, obviously accustomed to dealing with dazed family members. "She said she was Mrs. Starbuck's niece. Philadelphia," the nurse added.

The way she said it, Justin knew she meant to jar his memory. A name like Philadelphia would jar anyone, he thought. This Philadelphia woman was beginning to be a source of irritation. "Oh, she did, did she? And where can I find Niece Philadelphia now?"

The nurse looked at him as if she thought he was a little odd. "Probably in the lounge just beyond the doors you came through. It's to your right." She moved toward the doors herself and pointed.

Justin knew he was being dismissed. He let go of Rosalind's hand and took a step back. "Just one more thing. Who is my aunt's doctor?"

The nurse was already crossing to one of the cubicles. "Dr. Englund."

"Is he still in the hospital?"

The nurse nodded before disappearing behind a white curtain. "They can page him for you at the information desk, if you wish."

"I wish." He blew out a breath. There was no reason to be short with the nurse. This wasn't her fault. It wasn't anyone's fault. But he felt so damn helpless. He hated not having control, not being able to do something. "How is my aunt doing?" He addressed his question to the white curtain.

"Sir, you are going to *have* to leave." Then, because she understood, the nurse relented. "She's stable and was raising a fuss, so the doctor gave her something to make her sleep."

"That sounds like her." *Thank God*.

When he went in search of his new found "cousin," he was in a decidedly better frame of mind.

Until he saw her.

Philadelphia was sitting on the arm of a chair by the window, staring out at the parking lot below. She was disheveled, with long blond hair curling in every direction. And she was dressed in torn jeans and a sweatshirt that could have been inhabited by two of her. He guessed that she was slender beneath the baggy shirt.

He also guessed that she was some sort of a con artist. He had always thought of Aunt Roz as exceptionally shrewd, but the woman was getting on in years and when that happened, there was always the danger of vulnerability setting in. Con artists and people who ran scams thrived on vulnerability, feeding on it like vultures. Even pretty ones like this one. *Especially* pretty ones.

"So, I take it you're my long-lost cousin."

Philadelphia lost her balance on the arm of the chair and almost slid backward into the seat, her legs still slung over the side. Jumping to her feet, she pushed her hair out of her eyes and looked at him. She had been waiting to hear from Rosalind's doctor and was thrown off by this man and his manner. It was definitely not friendly.

"Excuse me?"

"My cousin. The nurse said that a Miss Jones, claiming to be Aunt Roz's niece, was sitting out in the lounge." He pretended to look around. "You're the only one out here."

His aunt. Well, that explained it. "You're Justin Starbuck." It wasn't a guess. He *looked* like a Justin Starbuck. Suit, three-piece, pressed, creases perfect. Nails short, straight, sandy-blond hair neatly cut, combed to perfection despite the windy morning. An unusually chiseled face, though. She would have expected a soft, pampered look, perhaps a rounded chin. But his face was made up of planes and angles. His looks would have improved immensely if he smiled. She wondered if he could.

Justin Starbuck quickly surmised this wasn't innocence personified before him. He'd bet his last dime on that. "I know who I am. The question remains, who exactly are you?"

"I already told you on the telephone when I called. Philadelphia Jones."

Philadelphia's spine stiffened. There had been no "thank you for calling me," no polite questions. He simply attacked. Just who did this man think he was?

All compassion evaporated. Philadelphia had a temper, and she felt it flaring. She drew herself up straight, trying to look him in the eye. She fell short by six inches. She should have grabbed her boots, not her moccasins, she thought. She didn't like the fact that he could look down on her. It gave him a psychological advantage.

"If you expect me to apologize for pretending to be your aunt's niece, I'm afraid you're going to be disappointed. It was the only way I could get in to see her."

Justin had to give her credit; she threw a good tantrum. He folded his arms before his chest. "And just why would you want to do that?"

So this was Rosalind's favorite nephew. The woman's taste needed improving. Philadelphia raised her chin. "I care about her."

"I see."

No, he didn't. He didn't see at all, she thought, judging by the look in his eyes.

He wondered if she always looked this appealing when she was disheveled and if this was the way she had gotten to his aunt. "How did you happen to find out that my aunt had a heart attack?"

Philadelphia fought the urge to turn her back and walk away without answering the condescending wretch. "I 'happened' to find out because I live with her."

"What? Since when?"

She was pleased that she had made him temporarily lose his cool. "Since I came to work for her."

This was all news to him. His aunt hadn't hired anyone new as far back as he could remember. He berated himself for not staying closer in touch this past year. The Foundation had been eating up more and more of his time since the plight of the homeless had become a national blight. "How long have you worked for her?"

She was beginning to feel as if she were under indictment, and guessed that was probably how he wanted her to feel. He didn't intimidate as well as his aunt did. But he did infuriate.

"Two weeks. I didn't bring on the heart attack, if that's what you're thinking." It was a flippant remark, but she felt like taking the shot. "Not a very trusting soul, are you 'Cousin' Justin?"

When she raised her eyes to his face like that, he could see flecks of amber in them. Like a cat. Cats were cunning. They were also sleek and sexy. He figured that she could be all three. What he couldn't figure out was why that interested him. "Trust is earned."

"Whatever happened to innocent until proven guilty?" she countered, growing amused. She needed her sense of humor. If she didn't use it, she'd probably punch his lights out in another five seconds. And from what Rosalind had told her, the woman was fond of Justin and undoubtedly wouldn't want him damaged. "You realize that you're looking at me as if you think I'm going to steal the family silver."

"Are you?"

"No. I don't care for the pattern."

"I see." He had expected huffy indignation, followed by denial, not wit. Despite himself, he was becoming just the slightest bit intrigued as to what exactly her game was.

For Philadelphia, it was a decided effort to hold on to her temper, and she wondered if it was worth the effort. Because Rosalind would have wanted her to, she tried again. "Would you like details?"

"That depends."

"On what?"

"On what you're referring to."

The details on knocking off the safe to your aunt's house, she thought, biting back the words. She stepped away from the window. She couldn't quite put her finger on why, but he made her feel cornered. What was this man's problem? Besides the paranoia of the rich, of course. She was well acquainted with that, thanks to Mark's mother.

Philadelphia pressed her lips together. "The way I see it, Mr. Starbuck, your only concern—a concern we share—is the condition of your aunt."

Rather than agree with her, he prodded her with another question. "Why isn't Angie here?" Someone from the house should have been here to handle things. Someone who knew his aunt, not this flighty opportunist.

"Because I didn't want two women with heart attacks on my hands. Angie was the one who found your aunt, and she took it very, very hard. I asked her to stay at home."

"You asked her?"

Sparks flashed in her eyes as she put her hands on her hips. "Yes, that's the proper alternative to ordering someone, an action I'm sure that you're more acquainted with."

Now she was defensive, and he could deal with that a lot easier than he could with amused wit. "Just who are you to be issuing orders?"

She raised herself up on her toes. If she could, she would have gone nose to nose with this pompous ass. "I don't issue orders. That's for your aunt to do. I said I *asked* Angie to stay at home. You don't listen very well, Starbuck, do you?"

He listened well enough to note that she had dropped the *Mister* before his name. It surprised him to discover that he liked the way she spat out his name. Apparently his aunt's situation had him more rattled than he had wanted to admit. "I'm listening, but I still don't hear what it is you do for my aunt."

"You mean besides robbing her blind and bilking her of her life savings? In my spare time, I'm her companion. I'm also helping her organize her notes so that she can get down to writing her memoirs."

"I didn't know she had hired a companion."

"Apparently there's a lot you don't know." Like how to be civil. Philadelphia told herself that she was just being edgy. Small wonder, considering the circumstances. The temper that was quick to flare was just as quick to disappear. She hated being angry. "Fortunately for you—" a smile rose to her lips "—I'm the forgiving type."

He found her smile bright, dazzling and just the tiniest bit unsettling. The last came from the fact that he didn't know what she was up to, he thought. "Which means?"

"Which means that I'm willing to forget about your show of ill temper and start over again." She saw Justin open his mouth to comment on her offer and held up a hand to stop him. "We're both a little overwrought here. We just show it differently. I talk fast, you bite off heads." She grinned again and stuck out her hand to him. "Care to start over?"

He took her hand mechanically. It was soft, surprisingly delicate. But her handshake was firm. If she were a con artist, he had the feeling that she was a wily one, and he began to wonder just what it was that he was agreeing to start.

Chapter Three

He was holding her hand too long.

Justin abruptly released it. For some reason, shaking Philadelphia's hand made him feel as if he was giving in to her. He had no intention of doing that. His suspicions about her were stronger than ever, despite the genial look in those green eyes of hers as she struck the bargain with him.

There was something about her that made him uneasy, unsure of himself. Uncertainty was not a familiar feeling for him. The mistake of looking into her eyes as he had taken her hand had been his undoing. They were large and green and so seemingly innocent. Yet, were they? Was she?

The waiting area was stuffy. The scent of rubbing alcohol wafting through the air was particularly pungent. Justin suddenly felt a need to clear his head. "I'm going to have Dr. Englund paged."

As he turned away, he was annoyed with himself for feeling that he needed to explain his actions to her. There was no need to tell this woman where he was going. He never explained himself to anyone. There had never been a need to do so. When he'd been a child, no one seemed to care what he was doing or where he was going. Certainly not his father or the ever-changing parade of stepmothers. Everyone had always been too busy to care. Except for Aunt Roz. And when he had become an adult, he had never seen the need to explain himself or justify his actions, not in his work or in his private life. Both his position in society and at the Foundation afforded him that luxury.

So why did he feel he had to tell this disheveled woman who looked as if she combed her hair with an egg beater where he was going? Why were those brilliant green eyes so hypnotic?

The rubbing alcohol, he reminded himself. Too many fumes tended to cloud the brain.

Backing away from the scent of the rubbing alcohol and Philadelphia, Justin realized that he didn't know where he was supposed to be going.

"I've already done that."

Justin paused to look at her, one eyebrow arched. She didn't look efficient. But she obviously seemed to be. Why did he find that irritating? He usually applauded efficiency. Maybe, he reflected, it was because he felt as if he was engaged in some sort of mental tug-of-war. And losing.

Philadelphia stuck her hands into her back pockets and returned his gaze. She couldn't shake the feeling that she was trapped under a glass, being carefully examined the way a butterfly might be by an entomologist. She didn't think she could put up with this for long. With any luck, Justin Starbuck would remember some pressing business elsewhere and be gone shortly. Rosalind had referred to him as a workaholic.

"You did, did you?" He didn't like being usurped. Rosalind had turned to him for advice and had looked to him to handle things for her since he had graduated college. She hated being bogged down with details. He enjoyed it. Justin felt more than a twinge of vexation that this woman thought she could just waltz in and take over.

Maybe he should be grateful to her. After all, he hadn't been here when she had done all this. But he wasn't grateful. He was annoyed. He caught himself wondering why he was being so unreasonable, but let it go.

Philadelphia ran her hands along her arms, wishing she had brought a sweater along with her. The hospital was chilly, but the critical look in Justin's eyes was heating her up quickly. "I did. He's your aunt's—"

"Doctor, yes, the nurse told me." Seeming to resign himself, he crossed back to her, the heels of his shoes hitting the checkered floor in a measured, rhythmic cadence that made Philadelphia think of a military step. "I suppose I should thank you."

"Don't bother. I wouldn't want you to choke to death." Her tone was purposely bright and breezy as she turned her face to look out the window. With determination, she tried to block him from her mind. Slowly, she began to count to herself. By the time she reached twenty-five, her pulse had settled down and she began to focus on the view.

One lone sunbeam had burst through a hole in the clouds and cast a rainbow through the window onto the floor next to where Philadelphia was standing. A bit of it caught in her hair. Justin hadn't the slightest idea why that seemed so picturesque to him or why he was certain that her hair, which looked even blonder the closer he was to her, smelled of wildflowers. Probably some popular perfume or maybe just her shampoo. Still, he found it somewhat... stimulating.

He shifted, trying to regain ground. He knew that he was annoyed with Philadelphia, but for the moment, he couldn't actually remember why. Then it came to him. "You take a lot upon yourself, don't you?"

Philadelphia turned. She was tired and hungry after the long ordeal. All she wanted was to lie down some place and sleep for a few hours, not thrust and parry with this man Rosalind prized, although heaven only knew why. The woman had called him "the only relative in this caldron of grasping relations in my life who is worth a damn."

If he was worth a damn, Philadelphia had yet to see it.

She bit her lip and told herself to give him another chance. After all, he *had* hurried to Rosalind's bedside. Maybe this was the way he handled stress. Well, that still didn't give him an excuse to be so damn rude.

"Starbuck." She raised herself on her toes once again. "What *is* your problem?"

Justin suddenly became aware of a rather amused-looking older man standing off to one side, observing them. Justin had been so engrossed in Philadelphia that he hadn't heard anyone approach.

Justin turned, about to extend his hand and introduce himself. He instinctively knew that this was Rosalind's doctor. The tall, white-haired man, however, was crossing to Philadelphia. "Miss Jones?"

To Justin's astonishment, Philadelphia transformed from a feisty firebrand to an anxious young woman right before his eyes. It reinforced his belief that she was only pretending to have Rosalind's best interests at heart.

Quite a chameleon, this one. His irritation mounted when he realized that the doctor was addressing her rather than him about his aunt's condition.

"How is she, Doctor?" Philadelphia was asking.

Justin noticed that her eyes were wide again and her hand was on the doctor's arm. She hadn't known the man for more than two minutes and she was acting as if they were intimate acquaintances. What kind of a woman had his aunt taken into her life?

Justin had always been suspicions of anyone who appeared so open, so friendly. Being suspicious was a trait he had acquired early. At least two of his stepmothers had acted just the way Philadelphia was before they had married his father. Justin had been taken in by them, only to learn that they were insincere, pretending to care about him, using him as a tool to prove their good intentions to his father when all they were really after was his father's money.

Time to take charge here before Miss Green Eyes mesmerized the doctor into forgetting his own name, Justin thought. Without realizing it, he put his hand on the doctor's other arm, much the way Philadelphia had, in an effort to draw the man's attention from Philadelphia, not from any desire to make contact. It was against his nature to do so. Communication was done verbally, not physically. But these were desperate times. He was fighting fire with fire.

"Dr. Englund, I'm Rosalind Starbuck's nephew Justin. Will my aunt be all right?"

A trace of reluctance was evident in Dr. Englund's eyes as he turned from Philadelphia to look at Justin. "She's a hard lady to keep down." The doctor's white moustache appeared thin above his upper lip as he permitted himself a smile. "Every bit as tough as I would have expected her to be. I saw her in *Champions All* a total of six times...." He sighed, a faraway look entering his eyes. "Well, never mind that." He waved a narrow, skillful hand at the thought. His expression changed, no longer that of a fan but of a cardiac surgeon. "I'd say that the danger has passed for the time being. But she is by no means out of the woods yet. The lady is going to need surgery, I'm afraid."

Justin knew this news wasn't going to please Rosalind. "What kind of surgery?"

Philadelphia noticed that his tone was suspicious again. Did he hold the whole world suspect? How awful for him. Or was it something else? Was he just hovering here because of his aunt's money? No. She didn't know why, but she had a feeling that this very stiff-necked man genuinely cared for Rosalind.

"At first," the doctor went on, "I was hoping that we might get away with just an angioplasty. We call it balloon surgery. Very simple, really, but quite effective."

In his heart, Justin knew he was grasping at straws. "Then why can't you . . ."

"Some of the veins have been damaged, making the procedure impossible. I'm afraid they're going to have to be replaced. All the tests aren't in, but I would say that from what I've seen, she is a major candidate for a triple bypass. You're free, of course, to get a second opinion, but I very much doubt that it will differ from mine."

Philadelphia sucked in her breath and raised her hand to her mouth to hold back a gasp.

Watching her from the corner of his eye, Justin thought she was simply acting again. But his conviction wavered. She really did look upset.

He glanced back to the doctor. She certainly had convinced the cardiologist. Dr. Englund seemed to totally block Justin out as he put his hand on Philadelphia's shoulder. "It's not as awful as it sounds, Miss Jones. The survival rate is high and getting better all the time. People with bypasses go on to lead very satisfying, active lives. Far more active," he emphasized, "than if they hadn't had the surgery."

"And if she doesn't have it?" Justin pressed.

The doctor's thin shoulders shrugged beneath the white lab coat. "She might go on indefinitely, and then again, she might have another attack, a fatal one. The best she can hope for without surgery is a life of inactivity."

That, Justin knew, would be worse than death to Rosalind. She thrived on being in the thick of things, on visiting her friends, on attending functions. She adored all the award ceremonies, presiding over them like a grand dame of the entertainment world. The only part she was never meant to play was that of a frail invalid. She'd never be able to carry it off.

There were no options, Justin thought grimly. She had to have the surgery.

"How soon will she have to have the operation?"

Philadelphia's question brought Justin back to the present. She was usurping him entirely. This was *his* aunt they were talking about, not hers. She had no right to take over this way. He had no idea what her true intentions were. He only knew what Rosalind meant to him. Everything.

Philadelphia was aware of the frosty glance Justin gave her when she talked to the doctor. She felt like giving him a swift kick. Later they'd battle it out as to who got to ask questions about Rosalind. Right now, she needed to know the facts. Rosalind had to be prepared for this, and Philadelphia had elected herself to do the job. Mr. Know-It-All probably had the beguiling bedside manner of a guerilla commando.

"Soon." Dr. Englund's expression softened at the worry lines crossing Philadelphia's brow. "As I said, Miss Jones—"

"Philadelphia," she corrected.

"Oh, for crying out—" Justin muttered, but if the doctor heard him, he gave no indication.

"Philadelphia," the doctor continued, "she's not in any immediate grave danger, but I wouldn't hold off too long," he advised. A high-pitched noise went off from the pocket of his lab coat. "My beeper." Dr. Englund dug deep into his pocket and produced the small black device. "If you'll excuse me. I'll see you later, Philadelphia." He gave Justin a perfunctory nod and left to find a telephone.

If he wasn't so concerned about Rosalind, Justin would have been considerably more irked. But if he let this episode pass without comment, there was no telling how far she'd go. "You really do take over, don't you?"

She had just about had it with this pompous so-and-so. Favored-nephew status or not, she was ready to let him have it. "Maybe if you asked questions a little faster, he would have directed his answers toward you. I think you should tuck your ego problem away until your aunt is better."

"Ego problem!" A nurse passed by them on her way into the C.C.U. area and gave Justin a funny look, but he was too provoked to care that his voice was several decibels louder than normal. "I don't have an ego problem."

"Right. I have it." Philadelphia turned from him and began walking toward the coronary-care unit. "I don't have to stand here and listen to this. If you'll excuse me—"

He took hold of her forearm. It didn't feel soft the way he had expected. There was strength there. She probably got it by throwing her temper around.

Philadelphia froze, then looked down at his hand until Justin removed it almost self-consciously.

"Where are you going?" His tone was purposely gruff to cover his unsettled feelings.

It was an effort for her not to yell at him, but she succeeded. "I'm going to find out if Rosalind has regained consciousness again. If she has, I'll go see her. If she hasn't, I'm going to call home and tell everyone the news."

Home. The word grated on his nerves. She was calling Aunt Rosalind's estate "home." As if it was hers. She worked fast. "I see. And while you're doing all this, what is it you want me to do?"

She didn't like the sarcasm. She wasn't at all sure she liked him, either. But she gave him the benefit of the doubt, considering the circumstances. A *slight* benefit of the doubt.

"Whatever it is you want to do." She had a few choice suggestions, but kept them to herself.

"You seem to be forgetting that Rosalind is my aunt."

"No one ever said she wasn't." Philadelphia crossed to the C.C.U. doors. They parted and she walked through.

He was exactly one step behind her. Not because he didn't want her getting the advantage, that was beside the point. The point was that he really wanted to see his aunt open her eyes and look up at him. If he had to endure having this exasperating blonde next to him to do it, so be it.

Everything would be all right if Rosalind just opened her eyes, Justin thought. He remembered that as a child, those wide, violet eyes had seen into his soul, made him laugh again when laughter was as remote to him as the stars in the sky.

The stars. Rosalind believed in the stars. He didn't, but right now, he hoped that if there were any truth to the theory that they determined destinies, that they had determined that her life was fated to be longer.

The same nurse he had encountered before was on duty. She was entering hourly statistics into the large log book that was on her desk. Frowning, the nurse directed her mild look of disapproval toward Justin. "I thought I asked you to come in one at a time."

Justin opened his mouth to respond, but Philadelphia spoke first. "Sheila," she said softly, looking around the immediate area, "there's no one else here right now. Please, no one'll mind if we see Aunt Rosalind for a minute. We just spoke to Dr. Englund."

The inference in Philadelphia's voice made it sound as if the doctor had okayed the joint visit. Justin knew that was what she was hoping the nurse thought. She was definitely devious.

"Well..." The young nurse pressed her lips together, thinking. She glanced up at the large clock that hung over the desk. "Just five minutes," she warned, relenting. "It'll be my head if anyone finds out."

"No one'll find out." Philadelphia held up her hand. "Scout's honor. Thanks, Sheila."

Justin slipped into Rosalind's curtained cubicle with Philadelphia. "You know her?" He nodded toward the nurse.

Philadelphia felt worry gnawing at her as she looked down at Rosalind. She barely heard Justin's question. "Who?"

"The nurse. You know her?"

"No."

That didn't make any sense to Justin. Philadelphia had called the woman Sheila. "But you know her name—"

Philadelphia glanced at him over her shoulder, her expression pityingly patient. It vexed him beyond words, and he had a feeling that she knew it.

"I can read."

He didn't want to argue with her, not here by his aunt's bedside, but it was happening almost against his will. "What does that—"

Philadelphia sighed, shaking her head. "Her name tag, Starbuck. I read her name tag."

He hadn't even noticed that the nurse was wearing one, but refrained from saying so. Somehow, he knew that admitting his oversight would give her another point in her advantage.

"People are friendlier if you take the trouble to learn their names. But I don't suppose you'd know that." To her mind, this man was a mountain of ice and needed someone to light a fire under him. She found herself volunteering for the job.

"So you've met."

The weak voice made them both swing their heads toward the pale figure lying in the bed. Justin was quick to take Rosalind's hand in his, his fingers wrapping around them protectively.

Philadelphia noticed the fear that passed through his eyes, even though his expression remained calm. *So, you do have feelings,* she thought. The realization heartened her more than she thought it would.

"Yes, we've met," he answered, glancing at Philadelphia. He struggled to keep the disdain from his voice. Nothing mattered except seeing Rosalind well again. But somehow, the sarcasm leaked out. "And you needn't worry. She seems to have taken complete charge of everything."

"Aries," Rosalind murmured.

"No," Justin corrected. "Philadelphia."

Rosalind tried to shake her head. It hardly moved. "Her sign. Can't help it."

Philadelphia touched the woman's shallow cheek lovingly. "The doctor's a fan."

"As well he should be," Rosalind answered, pleased.

Justin began to feel better. That spark he was looking for was in his aunt's eyes. "He says you're one tough old girl."

Rosalind frowned slightly. "Not old, Justin." She struggled to project her voice. It was hardly louder than a whisper. "I've a few years to go before I'm old."

"Sorry, lost my head." He grinned at her and squeezed her hand. "Never old, not you."

"That's better." Rosalind sighed. With considerable effort, she turned her head and looked at the paraphernalia attached to her. Tubes crisscrossed, meeting at junctions along her body. "God, I just look awful."

"You've looked better," Philadelphia said easily. She ran her hand through her own tousled hair. "We all have." Her innate thoughtfulness earned her a smile from Rosalind. Philadelphia glanced at Justin. "Except, maybe him." She leaned closer to Rosalind and lowered her voice only slightly, knowing he would hear. "Is he always so neat?"

Rosalind smiled. At least, Philadelphia thought she did. She knew Rosalind was trying to. "Always."

Justin didn't like being discussed. Having attention drawn to him always embarrassed him. He patted Rosalind's hand. "Look, save your strength, Aunt Roz—"

Rosalind sighed as she looked at Philadelphia with resignation. "He also likes to give orders."

Justin grinned at his aunt. "Runs in the family."

"I feel so sleepy," Rosalind confided, her voice low. She struggled weakly. "But I don't want to close my eyes."

Philadelphia understood her fear. "They gave you a sedative," she said soothingly.

"They would." The violet eyes were drifting shut. "Too much for them to handle—"

"You're too much for anyone to handle," Philadelphia said with a laugh. Rosalind's eyes opened again. Gratitude shone in them.

Rosalind shifted in the narrow bed, and Justin made a grab for an intravenous bottle that tottered dangerously. "Hey, easy there."

"When can I get out of here?" Rosalind struggled desperately against the drowsiness that was overtaking her again.

To Justin's surprise, Philadelphia looked toward him and inclined her head, as if urging him to answer the question. Was she actually deferring to him? He stared at her as Philadelphia nodded firmly, her eyes indicating Rosalind.

Rosalind caught the byplay and frowned. "Philadelphia, get me my clothes." There was alarm in Rosalind's voice.

Justin bent closer. "You can't go anywhere, Aunt Roz." He didn't know how to sugarcoat this. It was best to tell her straight out. She had always appreciated honesty. "They want to operate."

The sleepy eyes were forced open, the violet irises large. "My clothes," Rosalind repeated weakly. She tried to gesture, but her limbs were restrained.

"Do you want to go home first?" Philadelphia asked, sensing what was on Rosalind's mind.

Rosalind sank back against the pillow and sighed in relief. "Yes."

Philadelphia patted the woman's hand. "I'll see what I can do."

"Thank you." The words were barely out before Rosalind slipped into sleep.

"What do you mean, you'll see what you can do?" Justin's voice rose. Who the hell did she think she was, pretending to play doctor with his aunt's health, offering her false hope? She had nothing to say about the matter.

Philadelphia gave him a knowing look, and he realized that he had lost his temper. Again.

"Time's up," the nurse said sternly, appearing at the bedside.

"We were just leaving, Sheila," Philadelphia assured her, walking out. "And thank you."

The nurse nodded her reply.

Justin followed in Philadelphia's wake, hoping he could keep his anger in check until they were outside the unit's automatic doors. Ms. Philadelphia Jones, if that was her real name—and he had his doubts—needed some dressing down. And he was more than ready to take on the job.

Chapter Four

Justin managed to catch up to Philadelphia in the hallway beyond the waiting room. For a petite woman, she certainly moved fast. "Hold it a minute."

In an effort to stop her, he took hold of her shoulder. She kept making him react physically instead of intellectually, and he didn't care for it, but being physical with her was the only approach that worked. "Just who do you think you are, making decisions about my aunt's health?"

For Philadelphia, once her adrenaline was going, it was hard to stop. All she could think of was the terror in Rosalind's eyes when she heard the word *operate*. Didn't this man understand that? Didn't he *want* his aunt to feel better? She knew that by rights of protocol, she should step back. He should be the one taking charge, making whatever decisions needed to be made. After all, he was the blood relative here, although she had strong suspicions that mostly ice water ran through his veins.

But stepping back had never been Philadelphia's way. She felt it her duty to do what she thought was right. "We'll discuss my identity later. Right now, I want to find the doctor."

"Philadelphia." The absurdity of addressing someone by the name of a city hit him. "Don't you have another name? I feel like an idiot, calling you that."

"I don't think my name has anything to do with that state of affairs, Starbuck, do you?" She looked up at him, her bangs falling into her eyes, her smile challenging.

The idea of throttling her was beginning to present itself to him in a very appealing light. God, he was actually thinking in terms of violence. He hardly knew himself. But he wasn't going to let her get away with offering Rosalind false hope. His aunt had looked so frightened, it tore at his heart. He wasn't about to have her fear prolonged. "Just what do you mean, making my aunt think she can go home before the surgery?"

His eyes clouded to a terrifying dark gray when he was angry, she thought. Like Zeus on the mountain. But Zeus was too removed from humans and didn't understand what people needed. They had that in common, too. Couldn't he understand why Rosalind needed to go home, if only for a little while?

Philadelphia shrugged, the baggy sweatshirt sliding down one bare shoulder. Without thinking, she pulled the sweatshirt back into place. "Maybe she can."

Justin realized that he had been staring at her bare shoulder and redirected his gaze. That was probably done on purpose to distract him. Still, she had looked awfully sexy.... Damn, what was wrong with him? "That's ridiculous," he snapped, angrier at his reaction to her than what she was proposing.

Philadelphia sighed. Maybe he'd get the picture if she used shorter words. "Look, Starbuck." She spread her hands, and the sweatshirt slid off her other shoulder this time. "The lady is over seventy years old—"

Annoyed, Justin pulled up the sagging neckline on her sweatshirt. He couldn't concentrate, looking at her like that. "I know how old my aunt is."

He brushed his hands against her bare shoulder and watched her eyes open wide at his touch. She hesitated for a brief second, then continued, haltingly at first.

"Score one for you." She blinked. "The fact remains, she is over seventy and afraid that maybe she won't survive the operation."

Justin didn't want to think about what she was inadvertently suggesting. "The doctor just quoted figures..."

In one of her talks with Philadelphia, Rosalind had launched into her favorite topic, how people could be governed by their signs. She had used Justin as an example, pointing out how he tended to see the whole picture and forget about the small parts. "Typical Capricorn," she had said. Philadelphia was beginning to understand what Rosalind had meant. Maybe there was more to this astrology business than she had thought.

"Rosalind isn't a figure, a statistic. She's a person, a person with fears. You do know about fears, don't you, Starbuck?"

"Yes, I know about fears," he admitted before he realized it. He clamped his mouth closed for a moment, furious that he had let that slip. She had no business in his private life, in his past. "Don't preach at me...."

She opened her mouth, then shut it, then opened it again, deciding that silence wasn't going to work and besides, she had never been any good at it anyway. "I have no intentions of preaching at you, Starbuck. My only thought now is to talk to the doctor again."

"Why?"

Philadelphia rolled her eyes. Wasn't he paying attention? "To ask him if she can go home for a few days and prepare everything."

"What 'everything'?"

"I don't know," she fairly shouted, then stopped herself. She tried again, her temper in check, her voice subdued. She turned her face up to his, appealing to whatever feelings he might have. Part of her felt as if she was waging a losing battle. "Maybe she'd feel more up to the surgery if she tied up all the loose ends, saw her things again. Maybe watched an old movie of hers on video. Reread some old love letters. I don't know, *something* to put her in a better frame of mind."

It all sounded nonsensical to him. Every day they delayed the surgery might be crucial. "What good would—"

"A lot. Mental attitude has a lot to do with an operation's success."

"*Competence* has a lot to do with the success of an operation." He had no idea why he was standing there arguing with her. He could easily overrule her. And yet a small part of him thought that perhaps, just perhaps, she was right. Another part of him thought he had lost his mind.

Philadelphia threw her hands up in the air. "I have the strangest feeling that if I pricked you, you'd bleed motor oil or whatever it is that they use to make robots run. Don't you have a heart at all, Starbuck?"

There was a whole host of things he wanted to say to her. Such as that he had never met another human being he wanted to strangle so much in his life as he did her. And yet, he couldn't escape the feeling that this infuriating, fast-talking woman was right, that somehow she had hit upon the essence of what made Rosalind tick. His aunt *would* feel more confident facing the operation if she were allowed to go home first and see everything one more time. Although this woman irritated him, Justin couldn't argue with Philadelphia's logic.

He dropped the hands that itched to wrap themselves around her slender throat to his sides. ''C'mon,'' he urged her gruffly, ''let's go to the information desk and see if we can't have the doctor paged before he leaves the hospital.''

He began to stride toward the bank of elevators down the hall. Philadelphia had to move quickly to keep up with him, but she wouldn't for the world ask him to slow down. Victory tasted sweet, and she was suddenly feeling immensely magnanimous. Maybe this man had possibilities, after all.

''Rhonda said he wasn't due to leave the hospital until ten this morning.''

''Rhonda,'' he repeated. He jabbed the Down button for the elevator, then raised an eyebrow as he looked at Philadelphia. Her eyes were just level with his shoulder. ''Another name tag you read?'' he guessed.

''Another person wearing a name tag, yes.'' But she smiled as she said it. She leaned her shoulder against the wall and folded her arms, making no secret of the fact that she was studying him. Studying him intently.

''Trying to read my name tag?'' he asked with a touch of sarcasm that somehow was getting difficult to maintain in the face of her smile.

The elevator doors opened, welcoming them into a car that was almost filled to capacity. Justin hesitated, about to suggest that they wait for the next car to arrive. He never got a chance. Philadelphia grabbed his hand and pulled him inside just as the doors were closing. He found himself wedged uncomfortably against the wall.

And her.

"No," she answered much to his dismay now that there was an audience present. Obviously the woman didn't know the meaning of the word *private*. "I'm trying to understand why Rosalind is so crazy about you."

Several people turned his way and he tried to ignore them. He was more successful doing that than at ignoring her and the way her body felt against his. "I could say the same thing about you."

She laughed, her breasts moving against his chest. Something tightened in the pit of his stomach. "That's easy. I'm cheerful, helpful and I really love that woman."

She tossed words around too easily, he thought as the doors opened on the next floor. Yet another person entered. The sea of people pushed him tighter against the wall. She was pushed right along with him. Wasn't anyone getting off?

"That's impossible."

Her head nearly hit his Adam's apple as she looked up. He welcomed the distraction. "Why?" she asked.

He had always hated tight places. Justin tried to keep his mind on the conversation. It looked to him as if everyone else was, too. "According to your own admission, you've only known her for two weeks."

"Oh, I see."

He was getting to recognize and hate that knowing tone of hers.

"And you think love is as logical as a timetable. Week one, meet person. Week two, speak to person. Week twenty-three, ask person out for dinner."

She was making him sound like an idiot. Worse, she was doing it in a crowded elevator and didn't seem to mind that their conversation was being monitored by ten other people. She also seemed totally oblivious to the fact that their bodies were pressed together. Justin was now wedged in on one side by six IV bottles that were being transported to another floor by a very tired-looking orderly, the gun-metal gray elevator wall at his back and Philadelphia directly and totally at his front. In the old days, had their bodies been any closer together, there would have been reason enough for a shotgun wedding.

She might be unaware of their present, compromising position, but he wasn't. He was very aware of the fact that her soft contours were stirring him to a point to which he truly didn't wish to be stirred. At least, not by her.

He looked down at her, their faces almost touching. "You're completely infuriating, do you know that?"

"Nope."

His breath fanned her face and momentarily made Philadelphia grateful for the fact that the elevator had been this crowded. It felt nice. He might be pompous, annoying and pigheaded, but he certainly was a handsome, appealing man. It didn't erase his faults, but it did help blunt them.

"Well, let me be the first to tell you," he announced, "although I don't see how that's possible."

"It isn't. I'm not."

He wondered what in heaven's name she was babbling about now. "What?"

"No one is completely anything." She tried to turn and found that she couldn't. She heard the elevator door open behind her. Someone got off, and she almost pitched forward. This time, it was Justin who dragged her along.

Justin was relieved to get off the elevator. Two more minutes and his alarmingly physical reaction to her might have become evident to more than just him. Hands still linked, he pulled her along in his wake. "Well, then you'll have the honor of being the first. We can notify Ripley's Believe It or Not!"

The people who got off with them on the first floor seemed reluctant to leave the site of the discussion. Justin glared at them and pulled her aside.

"You're too uptight, Starbuck."

He glanced at her. "I wonder why that is."

"I haven't the foggiest."

"Look, let's just get to the information desk, okay?"

"Fine with me." As always, she led the way. And what was worse, he was beginning to expect it.

He caught up with her, deliberately pacing himself one step ahead.

Refusing to be baited, Philadelphia merely shook her head. "You really are too uptight, Starbuck. We're going to have to do something about that."

Quickly, they passed the gift shop and a wall covered with framed photographs heralding the hospital's past chairmen of the board. "I can think of one thing . . ." Justin eyed her meaningfully.

She merely grinned in response. He looked kind of adorable, she decided, with color rising in his cheeks. She gestured to a wide circular desk. "We're here."

"Thank God for small favors," he muttered.

Striding ahead of Philadelphia, Justin approached the pink-smocked volunteer sitting at the information desk. The white-haired woman looked up with a genuine kindly smile that Justin noted seemed to absolutely bloom when she looked past his shoulder. He didn't have to turn around to know that the woman was looking at Philadelphia. What *was* it about this woman that people took to so quickly? She was certainly rubbing him the wrong way. But then, he prided himself on not being taken in easily.

He had always thought of Rosalind in the same light. Still, advancing age did rob you of some of your mental faculties, he thought again. He promised himself to look into

Philadelphia's references as soon as possible. Finding none, as he felt certain that he wouldn't, he'd send the woman packing quickly. If his aunt really wanted a companion, he'd find a suitable one for her. She deserved the best, and that did not include a woman who came on like the U.S. Marines landing on the beach at Normandy.

"I'd like to have Dr. Englund paged," he told the woman. He glanced down at her smock and saw that her name tag did indeed read "Rhonda."

"Of course."

Justin realized that she addressed the words to Philadelphia, who had inclined her head sightly in support of his request. He wasn't used to needing someone to second his requests. He also wasn't used to having his emotions stirred up. Yet after only an hour in this woman's company, everything inside of him was in a state of total turmoil.

Dr. Englund answered his page via telephone. Justin held out his hand when the volunteer at the information desk announced that she had the doctor on the line. Obligingly, Rhonda handed him the receiver. Justin glanced at Philadelphia, who merely smiled at him. Maybe she was finally learning her place.

Justin was relieved to be allowed to conduct his conversation with the man alone. The relief was short lived, however. Philadelphia was not above coaching his end of the conversation from the sidelines.

She stood on her toes when Justin pulled back. "Tell him that it would do her health a world of good if she were allowed to go home for a few days before the operation."

Justin covered the mouthpiece. "I'm sure the doctor knows what's best for Aunt Roz's health better than—excuse me, Doctor?" He released his hold on the mouthpiece, acutely aware that he obviously hadn't covered it well enough. The doctor had heard what Philadelphia was saying and was addressing his answer to her suggestion.

The doctor's deep voice carried well enough for Philadelphia to pick up his answer. "As I said before, your aunt is in no immediate danger. I've found that it is in the patient's best interests to have them in as good mental spirits as possible. If going home for a few days will make your aunt feel more up to facing the surgery, I see no harm in it. You and your cousin can take your aunt home. Call my office later today and we'll make arrangements for admitting her for surgery later this week."

"Thank you." Justin replaced the receiver.

His cousin. He realized that he hadn't corrected the doctor about the fact that Philadelphia was in no manner, shape or form related to him. Well, no harm done. With any luck, he would have her out of his life shortly. Very shortly.

After his conversation with the doctor, Justin decided to tell his aunt the news. To his relief, Philadelphia, after borrowing twenty cents, elected to let him go alone, saying she wanted to call Angie with the news and check on someone named Ricky.

Ricky. Was that the name of her boyfriend? Would his aunt allow a live-in lover?

He turned for a moment just before he walked through the C.C.U. doors and looked at Philadelphia's departing figure. He wondered about the odd jealousy inside him as he contemplated her being with a lover.

Made no difference to him, he thought, giving the door an unnecessary shove as it sprang open.

Without even looking in the nurse's direction, Justin made his way to his aunt's bed. Rosalind's startlingly violet eyes tried to focus on his face as he took her hand in his. The grip was just the tiniest bit stronger this time. She was going to make it, he told himself.

"Thought you deserted me," she said weakly.

He hated the way the tubes made her look so frail. "Never." He saw the eyes move past him, searching.

"Where's Philadelphia?"

Justin tried to push aside his irritation. It wasn't his aunt's fault she had fallen victim to the hurricane-on-legs. "Calling Angie and checking on someone named Ricky."

"Good."

Good? Then she did know him. It was on the tip of his tongue to ask, but he didn't care who this Ricky was. All that concerned him, he told himself, was Roz's health. Not some fluffy blonde and her lover.

"I've got good news, Aunt Roz. Dr. Englund says you can go home for a few days."

"He has nothing to say about it." She wound her fingers around his, as if just now realizing that their hands were entwined. She tried to squeeze them, an entreaty in her eyes. "Come stay with me at the house, Justin."

Normally, she issued dramatic commands. He was used to that. He wasn't used to hearing a note of pleading in her voice.

He thought of the crammed calendar on his desk, the trip to Fresno this afternoon. The meetings set for the rest of the week. "Sure, I'll come." Somehow he'd find a way to make arrangements.

She sighed and nodded her head, pleased. "I want to go over my will."

Her request caught him off guard. "Why?"

"Justin, I'm not going to live forever."

"News to me." He raised her hand and held it in both of his. "Why don't we just get through this first and then we'll talk some more about your immortality?"

The lips that had once made a generation of men dream pulled into a faint smile. "You were always very good for me, Justin."

"Likewise, Aunt Roz." The words felt oddly rough in his throat. Justin made sure he maintained his smile. "Likewise."

She looked as if she was drifting off to sleep again. Her eyes closed, and her breathing became regular. He was content just to stand and look at her. But then the eyes opened again. Rosalind continued as if there had been no break. "How do you like Philadelphia?"

This question surprised him even more than her request for going over her will. He cleared his throat, looking for something neutral to say. "She's . . . interesting."

Rosalind smiled again, as if she knew something he didn't. Probably just the sedative, he thought.

"She's perfect, Justin." Rosalind moved her head slowly up and down. "It's in the stars." She was asleep again. He disentangled his hand slowly and slipped out quietly.

Turning to leave, he bumped into Philadelphia, who was standing on the other side of the cubicle's curtain.

Chapter Five

Their bodies touched, just the way they had in the elevator. Something hot and insistent shot through Justin with the sting of an arrow. He refused to acknowledge it. It was bad enough he had to acknowledge her. He wasn't a teenager held captive by his hormones. Why was he reacting this way? Especially with a woman he distrusted, a woman he found to be so different from everything he understood, everything that made him comfortable?

Justin stepped back. "And just how long have you been standing there?" His voice was harsh.

There was that grin again. He had hated it just a bit ago. Now he realized that when she grinned, her entire face lit up.

"Long enough to know that I'm 'interesting.'" Her eyes twinkled at him as she said it.

She had overheard. Justin didn't like invasions of privacy, even harmless invasions. And someone, a total stranger, capable of generating these physical feelings within him, was not harmless. "Do you always pry into people's personal lives?"

Small, shapely eyebrows disappeared beneath a fringe of bangs in a show of innocent surprise. "I don't call it prying."

"Oh, what do you call it?"

She glanced at the curtained cubicle. "Waiting my turn to talk to Rosalind."

He took hold of her elbow, escorting her through the doors. He was being physical again. It seemed to be the only way for him to be able to take charge with her.

Philadelphia started to protest, then thought better of it. She had to admit that she liked the feel of his hand on her arm. Anyway, letting the opposition think it had the upper hand was always a good ploy.

"She's asleep," he informed her.

Philadelphia couldn't resist a dig. After the anxiety she had been through all these long hours, she needed the release, however minor. "You do that to her?"

"The sedative—" he began to explain, and then stopped. Justin let go of her elbow. "Why are you deliberately trying to annoy me?"

In an odd sort of way, she liked him now, she decided. Things had seemed infinitely better since she'd learned Rosalind was going to be all right.

"I like watching the smoke coming out of your ears." She cocked her head, thinking the matter through. "And maybe it's a way of getting back at you for thinking I'm some sort of an opportunist. You don't seem to have a very high opinion of me."

Justin frowned. She made him feel like the villain in an old-fashioned melodrama instead of the sensible man that he was. Was undermining people's confidence in themselves the way she operated? "Should I have?"

She detected remnants of distrust in his eyes. That bothered her; she liked people to like her. "Your aunt does."

"My aunt seems to be a little befuddled." He could feel himself relenting despite common sense telling him otherwise.

"Oh, I wouldn't let her hear you say that." Philadelphia looked toward the C.C.U. entrance. "Heart attack or no, the lady would probably clip you one."

She turned her face up to his and laughed. Justin saw just the slightest hint of a dimple. It was near her eye. Even that wasn't usual. Nothing about this woman was orthodox.

"Of course, I'd volunteer to do the honors for her, seeing the circumstances."

"Of course," he echoed. He wasn't going to be drawn into another sparring match with her. "She asked me to stay at the house until after the surgery."

Philadelphia nodded. "I heard."

"And you heard my answer."

"Yes."

Of course she had. He was only grateful he hadn't said anything really private. "That means we're going to be running into one another." *Unless I can find a way to have you dismissed,* he added silently.

But Rosalind wouldn't hear of sending Philadelphia away. He knew that. Once you were part of her staff, you stayed. She was very particular about whom she hired. His aunt's judgments were quick, but motivated by some instinct that never failed her. Until now.

And then again, Justin thought, perhaps he was being too hard on Philadelphia. Well, hard or not, it was beginning to look as if he was going to have to put up with her for the duration. Thank God it was only a few days. He glanced at her and realized she was talking. She always seemed to be talking.

"Sure looks that way."

He made a decision for sanity's sake. "I'm willing to call a truce."

Philadelphia felt her temper rise, then recede in the face of amusement. The man probably didn't realize that he was being overbearing and sanctimonious. She pushed her sleeves up past her elbows. "Big of you, considering that you're the one who declared war."

Her smile, lopsided this time, made him pause. "Look..."

She threaded her arm through his and gave it her best shot. "This your way of maintaining a truce?"

Diplomacy was always a strong suit with him. Why was he coming up short here? He took a deep breath. "I think we're both agreed that we care about Aunt Roz's condition."

"Yes."

Her quick answer should have reassured him about her sincerity, but he kept feeling that he was picking his way through a maze. "Let's try to act civil around her."

"I don't need any lessons."

"Meaning I do?"

She smiled innocently again. "Did I say that?"

He decided the best way to deal with this woman was to get away from her. Disentangling himself from her arm, he moved ahead of her. "I'll see about having Aunt Roz discharged."

She knew he wasn't going to like this, but pleasing him wasn't her job. Or her avocation. And he'd be annoyed if she let him go through the trouble of walking down to the office after she had already made all the arrangements.

"'This afternoon at three, provided she comes out of her medication all right and doesn't take a turn for the worse,'"

Philadelphia quoted, calling after him. She braced herself for another volley of cryptic words.

He stopped, but didn't turn around at first. He needed a minute to compose himself. "You took care of it."

"I took care of it."

Competency had never annoyed him like this. Slowly, he rejoined her. "I can't find fault with your efficiency."

She could see saying that cost him. "But you'll try." She crossed her arms in front of her and tossed her head. Her bangs fell slightly to one side. She waited for the next salvo.

She had gotten the best of him again. He grinned unexpectedly and it made him look oddly boyish, a sharp contrast to the capable, tireless businessman.

"Hey, that's nice," she quipped.

His eyebrows drew together as Justin looked behind him to see what Philadelphia was commenting on. There wasn't anything there. "What is?"

"Your grin." She watched him sober. "Short-lived though it was."

Against his will, he was reacting to her remarkable expressions. Beneath all that wayward hair, there was a pretty face. What a pity that there was a mouth there, as well, he thought.

Justin glanced at his watch. The board meeting would just be winding up now. There were a lot of arrangements to be made and quickly, if he was going to be back here in time to take Rosalind home. He looked toward Philadelphia, who was oddly quiet for a change, watching him. He hated asking her a favor, then told himself that it was for his aunt's sake, not his own. And she *was* Aunt Roz's employee.

"Can you hold down the fort here for a few hours—or does Ricky need you?" Damn, where had that come from?

Philadelphia's breath caught in her throat. Why was he frowning when he mentioned her son? Didn't he like children, either? An image of a tow-headed, bright smiling face came to her, and she smiled without realizing it. Everyone loved Ricky, even when he was being cranky. Yesterday had been one of those days, but that was because he had the sniffles. She hoped that Angie could hold out with him just a while longer.

"No, Ricky's fine. He's not at the impatient stage anymore. He can cope for a few more hours."

Justin had a mental image of a tall, rugged-looking ape of a man grabbing Philadelphia as soon as she walked through the door and rushing off with her to their room. She made it sound as if he demanded regular attendance. Well, why should he care? And why was he so damned testy all of a sudden at the very idea that a man—

"Fine," he snapped. "Then I'll be back at the hospital at four. Wait for me."

She had never liked being ordered around. A request was one thing; being ordered around was something else again. If they were going to get along, he was going to have to learn the difference. "That depends entirely on Rosalind."

"Wait for me," he repeated deliberately.

Philadelphia bowed from the waist the way a slave might have. "Yes, sir."

Justin swallowed hard. The shapeless sweatshirt belied her figure. The movement of firm, full breasts could be discerned beneath the baggy material. She wasn't wearing a bra, he suddenly realized. Justin had a sudden urge to wipe that smile off her face with his own mouth. It wasn't like him. "See you at four," he mumbled.

As Justin left quickly, he wondered if burnout could happen to a man without his knowing it. After Rosalind was back on the road to recovery, he was going to take an extended vacation.

* * *

"Do you think anyone knew I was at the hospital?" Rosalind mused, reclining against a mountain of pillows that were arranged along one side of the stretch limousine.

"Knew? Cleopatra had less fanfare coming into Rome than you did leaving the hospital," Philadelphia commented with a laugh as Mallory pulled the limousine onto the long, serpentine driveway.

When they had made their exit from the hospital, Rosalind, sitting back in her wheelchair and feeling infinitely better, had insisted on going through the halls slowly, waving to anyone who stopped and stared, trying to place where they had seen the woman before. Her movie career had ended some fifteen years ago, but since that time, Rosalind had not gone into hiding. She attended fund raisers, chaired charitable organizations, gave interviews. Her face, by the virtue of celluloid and modern communications, was available to people of all ages. Nothing cheered her more than recognition, even though she pretended it didn't matter in the slightest.

Philadelphia noticed how the older woman thrived on attention and fawning fans. Rosalind might act indifferent, but she ate this up. Philadelphia wondered if the press had found out about her condition yet. Cards from well-wishers would do Rosalind a world of good.

"I played Cleopatra once," she told Philadelphia.

"I know."

The matter-of-fact way Philadelphia said it pleased the older woman. She looked at Justin. "I told you she was a find."

"Yes, a find."

Philadelphia caught the sarcastic tone and gave him an amused smile, but her mind was on the press release she had suddenly decided to issue.

She looked preoccupied, Justin thought. What was racing through her mind now? All the way home, he had been silently studying Philadelphia, watching her radiate within the dark interior of the limousine. No one, he noted, seemed unaffected by her. Not the volunteers at the hospital nor the nurses they dealt with while getting Rosalind ready for the trip home. Even Mallory, always so dignified, had made a visible effort to suck in his ever-expanding waistline when Philadelphia bounced into view.

The woman was too loud, too friendly, too everything, Justin concluded. Why the hell was that so appealing—to others, he amended mentally, and then wondered why he had been so fast to make that distinction in the privacy of his own mind. And what made him so nervous about her? He was never nervous.

The limousine came to a halt before a three-story house that belittled the word *mansion*. Its wings were wide, sprawling, larger-than-life, like the owner herself. After her husband had died, Rosalind had doubled the house in size. The expansion had eliminated much of the grounds, but that hadn't troubled her. Rosalind had never cared much for the outdoors.

"I hate this thing," Rosalind declared as Mallory brought around the wheelchair for her. Leaning heavily on Justin, Rosalind eased herself into it.

"Think of it as your chariot," he soothed.

"Then it should be of gold," she pronounced, vexed.

"We'll work on it," Justin promised.

Philadelphia noticed that it was Justin, not Mallory, who pushed the wheelchair through the front entrance. It was a thoughtful thing to do, she mused, her opinion of Justin going up a notch.

He caught the approval in her eyes as he passed, and he frowned.

It was a scene out of an old-fashioned movie, Philadelphia thought as she entered the house. The household staff was lined up in the foyer to greet the returning empress.

"Oh, Miss Roz, you gave me such a scare," Angie breathed, hurrying forward. She was a tiny woman with white hair that was pulled up in a severe knot on top of her head. She was married to Mallory and, from what Philadelphia could see, utterly dominated the man.

Rosalind was touched at the show of concern, but pretended to shrug it off. "You always did frighten easily, Angie. Such a mouse. As you can see, I'm fine." Rosalind glanced down at the wheelchair with a trace of annoyance. "Well, almost fine."

Angie looked to Philadelphia, who slowly shook her head, knowing that the woman would refrain from asking any more questions. Philadelphia had telephoned Angie earlier, telling her what the doctor had said about Rosalind's condition. Rosalind loved attention, but it was evident that she didn't want anyone fussing over her because of her bad heart. She had always been contemptuous of weakness, and to be ill was to be weak.

Rosalind looked down again at the wheelchair. "Not much like a barge, is it?" she asked, alluding to Philadelphia's reference to Cleopatra.

"Oh, I don't know," Philadelphia answered. "Movies are all make-believe, right?"

Justin looked at Philadelphia over his aunt's head. Much as he wanted to deny it, even this short exchange between her and his aunt showed him that she understood how the woman's mind worked. She seemed to instinctively know exactly the right thing to say. To his aunt.

This, of course, he thought as he pushed the wheelchair toward the elevator, did not automatically mean that Philadelphia *wasn't* a con artist. Quite the opposite could be true. He'd just have to watch her more closely. The prospect of doing that was not without its merits.

The rest of the household staff, the maid, Margarita, and Johann, the gardener, both looked relieved to see their mistress return so quickly. The hurried early-morning departure by ambulance had had them all fearing her demise.

"I pray for you," the maid said, a heavy Spanish accent clinging to each word.

"Pray for the doctor instead," Rosalind retorted with a wave of her hand.

The flare was back, Justin thought, savoring his aunt's dramatics. He thought that her answer wasn't that far off the mark.

"Mama!"

Justin stopped abruptly as a little boy with blond hair came running out of nowhere and wrapped himself around Philadelphia's leg.

She had a child.

The startling thought occurred to him just before the realization that she was married. Or was she? He had already assessed that she wasn't wearing a wedding ring. Maybe she was divorced.

Philadelphia dropped down to one knee and scooped up the boy into her arms. She nuzzled him in greeting, then kissed his head. "Hiya, Ricky. Were you a good boy?"

The blond head bobbed up and down hard. Philadelphia plucked a handkerchief out of her back pocket and remedied his running nose with a quick movement of her hand.

"No trouble at all, Philadelphia," Angie said proudly. "I kept him inside, just like you said."

The fact that Angie responded to Philadelphia as if she was in charge of the household instead of being the interloper was not lost on Justin. How tightly had this woman woven her web in two weeks?

He looked at the boy who wound his little arms around Philadelphia's neck. "*He's* Ricky?"

Philadelphia was too happy to be home again to do anything but say yes.

Justin took a deep breath. Then she was living here with her son and not her lover. And she wasn't married. He hadn't the slightest idea why a sense of depression was being lifted from him.

"Are we going to stand in the middle of the foyer, talking all afternoon?" Rosalind demanded. "I want to go to my room and put on something decent. Who picked this caftan, anyway?"

Margarita suddenly turned beet red. "I found it in the back of the closet."

"There's a reason for that. I don't wear peach in June." Rosalind caught Justin's expression in the mirror that hung over the dining room table as he began pushing her toward the elevator again. "Don't smirk. I have my reasons."

"The stars," he guessed fondly.

She nodded sharply. "They haven't failed me yet."

Philadelphia pressed the elevator button. The decorative door opened instantly.

"Here," Angie said, taking Ricky's hand. "He was about to help me with the chocolate pudding, weren't you Ricky?"

"Chocolate," Ricky echoed happily.

Philadelphia gave Angie a grateful smile. She wanted to see Rosalind settled in, then get a hot shower. She felt as if she had been running madly since early morning. "Bless you," she mouthed.

"I come along to help," Margarita volunteered, joining them before the elevator. She was a tall, stocky woman with a gentle manner and had, after Angie, been on the staff the longest.

The elevator closed. There was silence except for the whine of the motor. When the elevator stopped on the second floor, to Justin's surprise, Margarita looked at him inquiringly, then positioned her hands on the back of the wheelchair. Justin nodded and stepped back.

Rosalind straightened a little in the confines of her chair. "Well, what are you waiting for?" She glanced back at Margarita. "Get a move on, girl. I'm a very tired woman who's lucky to be alive."

A moment before, Rosalind had never been better. No one knew how to milk a situation better than Rosalind, Philadelphia thought.

She began to follow the small group down the hall, when a hand on her shoulder stopped her. She turned around to find Justin looking down at her. "Why don't you go change? You must be exhausted."

The display of consideration brought a smile to her lips. "As a matter of fact, I am. Are you being nice, Starbuck?"

He wasn't sure if she was teasing or being sarcastic. With her, he wasn't sure about a damn thing. Except that her smile was getting to him. The shape and curve of her mouth was getting to him.

"Yes."

"Oh." Philadelphia pretended to roll his answer over in her mind. "I wasn't sure. I thought maybe you were afraid that I'd steal your aunt's gold fillings when she's asleep."

"Do you enjoy being irritating?"

"I don't know." Her smile flashed again. Her teeth were even, dazzlingly white and perfect. "Let me explore it a little more."

"Then explore this while you're at it."

Suddenly, it was too much, the light scent tickling his senses, the teasing mouth curved up toward him, the demands that ran through his own body. He had no idea what came over him. Relief at his aunt's recovery. Overwork. Voodoo. Maybe all three. Maybe it was the narrow hallways. He had never done well with claustrophobia. It made him react strangely. Like now.

He had no idea why he kissed her. No idea that he was *going* to kiss her.

Until he did.

Somehow, her hair found its way into his hands, her body found its way against his and his mouth met hers as if it had been magnetized to do so.

Justin might not have understood what had pushed him to this point, but he did know one thing: he enjoyed kissing her. More than he knew he should.

Her mouth, so quick when forming words, was hot and just as quick beneath his. Each movement of her lips fanned something within him that had been smoldering all day, ever since he had first seen her. How could anything so irritating taste so delicious? Her mouth was like a feast, a cornucopia of tastes and secrets and promises. God, there were promises there. Things that told him that this was only the beginning. He felt his pulse racing and his mind blanking out as every other sense focused in on Philadelphia.

Alice had probably felt like this when she fell down the rabbit's hole, he thought. Except that Alice hadn't kissed the rabbit.

Chapter Six

He felt the way he had once when he was much younger and had fallen off the diving board into his aunt's pool. He had hit the water stomach first and all the air had been knocked out of him. This kiss had the same impact. Mallory had pulled him out then. There was no one to pull him out now.

Philadelphia was conscious of forcibly coming up for air. She opened her eyes, dazed, disoriented. And happy. Very, very happy. The smile she gave him rose up from her very toes. "Wow."

Drop your hands, Justin. Let go of her.

The command did not seem to register, for his hands lingered on the inviting curve of her waist, keeping her body against his for a few precious seconds longer. He stared down at her face, thinking that he was losing his mind. But there was a lot to be said for this kind of madness. "I don't know what came over me."

She didn't want to sound breathless, but it wasn't easy. "I'm not complaining."

If he apologized for this, she'd cut his heart out. Philadelphia hadn't felt this wonderful in a long time. After Mark had gone back to his mother's purse strings, she had cut herself off from all entanglements and concentrated on having and raising Ricky. When she had read about Mark's accident last year, she had felt strangely hollow, empty, but not affected. She had thought that meant that something had died within her. It was nice to know it hadn't.

Philadelphia wondered what Justin would say if she told him that he was the first man she had kissed in over two years. "I take it you're the type who believes that actions speak louder than words."

This time, he did release her. Having nothing else to do with his hands, he shoved them into his pockets, a habit he had always frowned on. "I didn't mean—"

"To kiss me?" She ran her fingers along her lips. "You could have fooled me. It certainly felt as if you meant to."

Witch's eyes. She had witch's eyes that laughed as she spoke. Were they laughing at him? Did she see how deeply that kiss had unsettled him? "I, umm—"

"Don't worry, I didn't take that to mean that you're madly in love with me, or even approve of me. But it was nice. Very, very nice." To punctuate her words, she rose on her toes and brushed his lips lightly with her own. Then she walked off, leaving him dazed in the aftermath and wondering what the hell had happened to make him go off the deep end like that. Tarzan would have displayed more finesse.

Justin wouldn't think about her. He had many more important things to be concerned about. Yet he felt dazed, as if he were sleepwalking. He found himself constantly losing his train of thought. Through his contacts at the phone company, he had had another line put in at Rosalind's estate that afternoon. He could stay as long as Rosalind needed him. All his calls were being transferred to the new number. He had his PC and his fax machine. There was no earthly reason why he couldn't function as well as he always did.

Except for one thing. A woman with a ridiculous name and lips that were impossible to forget.

The phone in his room rang incessantly. Each shrill ring burst upon him like a wave of cold water, bringing him back to reality. Reality fought for space with the memory of the delicious imprint of Philadelphia's mouth on his. It was like discovering a new flavor of ice cream that no one else knew about. He had always had a weakness for ice cream.

Feeling revived, her hair pinned haphazardly with wisps falling riotously about her face and neck, Philadelphia set about restoring order in her routine. Making sure that Rosalind had everything she might need within reach, she cajoled her into resting. Rosalind offered only token resistance before acquiescing to Philadelphia's tactful suggestion that she spend the next few days in bed.

"All right, I'll stay in bed." Rosalind accepted the remote control for the wide-screen television that took up part of one wall. "But just for tonight."

"One night at a time." Philadelphia winked as she handed her the television guide.

A wicked chuckle met her words. "That's what I used to tell all my men."

She must have been something else when she was young, Philadelphia thought. The stories she had read about Rosalind were probably only the tip of the iceberg. "I bet you did.'' Philadelphia only hoped she'd have that much spirit when she was Rosalind's age.

Rosalind thumbed through the guide, but she was showing signs of fatigue. ''How's Ricky doing?''

It touched Philadelphia that in the midst of her own problems, the woman expressed concern for her son. ''His cold is in the sniffling stage. With luck, it won't be anything else. Right now, he's glued to the television set. I want to thank you again for having that cable station hooked up.''

Rosalind, her eyes fighting to close, waved away the thanks. ''Keeps him from jumping up and down on my furniture,'' she mumbled just as she dozed off.

Angie walked in, a tray in her hands. The woman looked uncertainly at Philadelphia. ''How is she?''

''She just fell asleep. I don't think she'll be wanting that right now.'' Philadelphia moved quietly to the door.

''Fine thing.'' The dishes on the tray rattled as Angie turned around. ''You cook, you slave, trying to make things they'll like, and then they fall asleep on you.''

''Put it in the refrigerator.'' Philadelphia eased the door closed as Angie crossed the threshold. ''She's bound to want it later.''

''Yeah,'' Angie sniffed. ''When I'm asleep.''

''I can get up and—''

Angie gave her a sharp look. ''And heat up my soufflé?''

Philadelphia raised her hands in the air. ''Sorry, lost my head.''

The white head nodded smartly. ''Touch my soufflé and you will.''

''I'll keep that in mind.''

The older woman was appeased. ''Want dinner?''

Philadelphia glanced at Justin's door. The sound of his voice, low and unmodulated, drifted through the hall. He was on the phone again. It was past seven. How long did that man intend to work? "Not just yet. I'll help myself later."

"Huh!"

Philadelphia knew how Angie felt about people puttering in her kitchen. That the woman allowed her to do it at all was a coup. "You get some rest."

"Not with Mallory around, I won't. Man always has something he wants me to be doing." Angie ambled off, the sound of her footsteps gradually fading away down the hall.

Philadelphia shook her head. She knew that of the two, Angie ruled the roost. There was precious little Mallory could get her to do that she didn't want to do. That wasn't the way Philadelphia wanted it for herself. She wanted a partnership, straight down the middle.

The thought brought a smile to her lips. She knew she had a tendency to take charge without even realizing it. Her partner in life would have a strong personality to keep her from racing ahead.

Justin's voice caught her attention again just as she was about to go to the large TV room downstairs. She had left Margarita with Ricky watching a *Sesame Street* special. Margarita had seemed every bit as enthralled as the child.

Philadelphia crossed to Justin's door. Maybe he was hungry. She raised her hand, about to knock, then decided to wait until he finished his phone call. But she knew if she walked away and returned later, she'd find him on the phone again. Except for a brief visit with Rosalind, he had been on the phone for most of the evening.

As Philadelphia stood and listened now, she frowned. His voice sounded so cold, so detached. It belonged to a man who was the total antithesis of the one who had kissed her. More importantly, so different from the man she had heard talking to Rosalind. Where was his compassion for these people? She knew he was the head of a foundation that oversaw the distribution of funds to the homeless. That required compassion, didn't it? Where was his? He sounded more like a general issuing orders to his troops.

Philadelphia sighed. She supposed she was too sentimental to handle something like that on such a large scale. She had no head for cold, hard facts. If she were head of his organization, she'd probably wind up giving the money away to the first dozen needy people who approached her. Mark had called her hopelessly irresponsible. She had always thought of herself as kindhearted.

The word irresponsible hovered on her mind. In the end, it had been Mark, and not she, who had been irresponsible. He had left her while she was still pregnant, left her to have and raise Ricky by herself while he turned his back on their very existence. She supposed that she owed his mother a debt of thanks for having let her see Mark's true colors before it had been too late. She smiled. They didn't make thank-you cards for that sort of thing yet.

The sound of the receiver meeting the cradle brought her around.

She moved quickly, knowing that if she didn't, she'd be stuck out in the hall all night. She knocked and the door moved under her hand, opening farther. She pushed it all the way.

Justin looked up, only slightly surprised. Part of him had been expecting her to show up all evening.

"Hungry?"

"Yes." The word escaped without his conscious knowledge and he hoped she didn't take the response in the way he had meant it. He *was* hungry, hungry for a repeat serving of what he had sampled in the hallway. It was the main reason why he had all but sequestered himself in his room, burying himself in his work, hoping to bury a raw reaction to a woman he had no desire for. Desire. Oh, God, he *did* desire her.

Justin cleared his throat, aimlessly rifling papers on his desk. Too late, he realized that he had shuffled two separate files together like playing cards. He'd have to sort them out later. Damn her. "I mean—"

Philadelphia fought to control a grin. Was that color creeping into his face? Why was he embarrassed about being hungry? He was, after all, human. That episode in the hallway had proven that to her with the utmost satisfaction. "Ricky and I are going to have a light supper. If you'd like to join us..."

He looked down at his work, hoping she'd go away. "Just have Angie send something in."

"A can of oil, perhaps?"

He looked up. "What?"

Philadelphia moved effortlessly into the room. "A can of oil," she repeated, and picked up several papers that were spread over his desk and began to make a neat pile. "Robots need to be lubricated once in a while, so I'm told."

He took hold of her wrists. "Put those down, please." Belatedly, he realized that he was touching her again. Physical contact with her was something he was determined to avoid. Undemonstrative by nature, he had already touched, held and kissed her in less than a day's time. She had trampled on his independence and thrown his protocol into chaos. Being around her was turning him inside out.

She placed the papers on his desk. But she didn't leave, as he wished she would. Instead, Philadelphia looked around. He watched her gaze as it literally jumped from place to place. The bedroom was dark and masculine, with gray-blue walls and heavy mahogany furnishings. There was no place for light, airy perfume. Stirring perfume. Yet the room was suddenly filled with it. With her.

The room was too oppressive for her taste. She would have chosen something far more uplifting as far as furniture went. "Looks to me like you'll wind up with cabin fever if I leave you in here a minute longer."

"Where I stay is not a concern of yours."

She leaned her hip against his desk, oblivious to the dismissal in his voice. "Are you always this obstinate?"

"Are you always this pushy?"

She bit her lower lip and grinned, looking more like a mischievous little girl than a woman with a child. "No, I vary to fit the situation." She moved her fingers along the top of the PC on his desk. "This one's a toughie."

He found her grin irresistible and told himself that nothing would really be forfeited if he relented. After all, he did have to eat. "If I agree to have dinner, will you be quiet?"

She tilted her head to one side, pretending to consider the question. "I could try."

He liked the way her eyes danced when she teased. That was his first clue that he was coming unhinged. Had he been more observant, he would have realized that his undoing was not that far behind. Later he would trace it back to the moment he kissed her but for now, he was still mildly certain that if he went along with things, he could call the shots. "Not good enough."

She shrugged, drifting to the door. "'Fraid it's the best I can do."

Justin sighed, rising. "I guess I can't ask for miracles."

"Sure you can." When he joined her, she linked her arm through his. "Just don't be overly disappointed if they don't come on command. Miracles take time."

He had the strangest feeling she was putting him on notice as she smiled up into his face.

* * *

As long as he could remember, Angie had presided over

the kitchen with an iron spatula. Even Rosalind rarely interfered, letting the housekeeper have her way. It was what Justin was used to, what he expected.

When they entered, Angie mumbled a few words, then shuffled out of the way, warning them not to upset her soufflé. Justin was aware that he was staring at the exchange, dumbstruck.

"What's the matter?" Philadelphia placed Ricky at the table and spread his coloring book and crayons in front of him. His favorite toy, Mr. Tiger, was given the seat next to him and limply fell over. Ricky jammed the toy behind him and against the back of the chair, then began to color.

"I always thought Angie would defend this turf with her dying breath." Justin took another long, hard look at Philadelphia, trying to unlock the puzzle that was within.

"She knows that puttering around the kitchen relaxes me." Philadelphia rummaged through the refrigerator until she found the two steaks Angie had set aside for her.

He recalled all the times he had been summarily ushered out of the kitchen by Angie. Whatever magic Philadelphia was weaving, it was strong. "Want me to do anything?"

Philadelphia bit her lip. *Yes, hold me again the way you did before.* "You could make sure that Ricky doesn't wander off," she answered casually as she threw the steaks on the grill.

He looked over at the little boy. Ricky was wiping his nose with his sleeve. Mechanically, Justin took out his handkerchief and finished the job for him. Ricky tolerated it, then grinned.

He smiled just like his mother, Justin thought. Where was the father? Why was she here, alone? Who the hell *was* she?

Ricky returned to his coloring book, taking delight in creating swirls of purple on every inch of the page. Then, with a mild complaint, he stopped and held up his crayon to Justin.

He blinked. "You want me to color with you?"

The question surprised Philadelphia, and she turned. Her smile broadened. "I think he wants you to peel back the paper on the crayon. He can't draw anymore. Gets frustrated easily."

He could definitely relate to that, Justin thought, at least in the last few hours.

Twenty minutes later, she was serving dinner. Steak and salad. In place of salad, Ricky had reheated mashed potatoes. Justin had intended to eat and go, but it couldn't be done. He eyed Ricky, who sat at his mother's side, trying to flatten his potatoes and turn them into soup before he ate them.

"So where's your ex-husband?" Justin tried to sound disinterested. He waited for her answer, wishing it didn't mean anything to him. But it did.

"I don't have an ex-husband." For all the emotion there, she could have been saying that she didn't have a screwdriver. "Is your steak rare enough?"

He couldn't determine what her feelings were. For once, the face that had been so devastatingly expressive was totally unreadable. Except for that slight trace of wariness that had passed through her eyes when he asked. Or was that just his imagination? Was she really what she seemed, a single parent trying to make a living for herself and her son? Or was there more to it? And what about this ex-husband who wasn't?

"The steak is perfect. Did Ricky's father leave you?"

It was a blunt question, but he was hoping to catch her off guard to see some sort of reaction. He was disappointed. She didn't respond immediately. Instead, she raised her eyes to his in a fashion that he had, in the space of less than a day, come to know and look forward to even as he dreaded it. Dreaded it because something happened to his stomach when she looked at him like that.

"Personal questions, Starbuck?"

She was still hiding her feelings behind an act. He shrugged. In reality, it was no business of his if the man was Bluebeard. "Idle conversation."

"Oh. Well, since we're speaking idly," she said, her voice rising just a shade from its normal low, whiskey-soft range, "Yes, he did. That's very astute of you."

She didn't add that Mark had left because, failing to bribe her, Mrs. Mark Powell III had seen fit to threaten Mark IV with being cut off without a dime if he stayed with Philadelphia. Her pregnancy had never been an issue. Mrs. Powell had blatantly stated that the baby probably wasn't Mark's anyway. That had been when Philadelphia had lost her temper and thrown the woman out. Mark had left shortly thereafter. Permanently.

Philadelphia took a deep breath and let it out slowly. "I take it you guessed that because you think that any man in his right mind would run from me."

The flippant comment made him smile, and he did little to hide it. "Fast and to the hills."

Philadelphia looked at him intently, a knowing smile on her lips. "You're not running."

Something dark and hungry pulled at him. "We're not involved." He looked down at the steak with feigned interest.

"Aren't we?" she asked quietly.

He had never been a coward. Until this moment. But he refused to be backed into a corner. "If you're referring to what happened in the hallway—"

"I am."

He put down his knife and fork, no longer interested in pretending to be hungry. "You were the one who said you weren't going to construe that to mean anything."

She grinned. He was interested, and they both knew it. "Those weren't my exact words."

He leaned forward, his eyes meeting hers across the small kitchen table. Ricky whacked down another potato ridge with his spoon. Justin flinched at the sound. Philadelphia didn't seem to hear it. "You talk so much, how can you possibly remember your exact words?"

"I remember," she replied simply. "Eat your peas, Ricky."

She was maddening, absolutely maddening. And he had the awful, nagging suspicion that if he didn't put a stop to this, whatever "this" was, he was going to find himself in a position he had always vowed he'd never be in.

He had spoken to Dr. Englund's office and arranged for Rosalind to enter the hospital on Saturday. Maybe he could move that date up. The sooner Rosalind had her operation and was on the road to recovery, the sooner he'd be back in his office and away from this smug, self-satisfied, know-it-all woman who was already his own personal obsession.

"I heard you on the phone a little while ago," she said, abruptly changing the subject. Ricky sneezed, and they both chorused, "Bless you" at the boy, who found that riotously funny. "Sit up, Ricky, before you slide under the table."

No sooner had she said that, than he did, dragging his faithful tiger with him. Philadelphia shrugged and let the boy win the round.

Justin thought of the governesses who had marched through his life, beginning at around Ricky's age. They would never have let him get away with that. Discipline, nothing but strict discipline, had shaped his life in his father's house. There hadn't been room for leeway. Or love.

"You were saying?" he prodded.

"About what?"

She had the attention span of a sock, he thought, trying very hard to find things about her that annoyed him. "About listening in on my conversation."

Philadelphia ignored the little dig. "Oh, that's right. I was wondering— Finished?" She nodded at the plate.

"Yes." He frowned. How could she carry on three conversations at once?

She removed his plate and went on without skipping a beat. "How can you be head of something so noble and yet sound so remote, pretend to be so removed?"

"I'm not pretending."

She put the dishes into the sink and turned around to look at him. "Then you do have ice water in your veins? I don't think so."

"What you think really doesn't matter." He was annoyed that she was sitting in judgment of him. He had no way of knowing that she was always this open with her thoughts. "And to answer your question, I've rarely met individuals who merit compassion on a one-to-one basis. For the most part, people are greedy, cruel, selfish and grasping."

She stared at him. "Someone must have hurt you once very, very much."

She was too close too fast, and he didn't like it. "No one hurt me."

She looked at him more closely. He was protesting too much. She didn't believe him, but let the matter drop. At least that part of it. Whatever had happened, his view of the world was much too grim and depressing for her. "Why bother with the foundation if you feel this way about people?''

"Because poverty is obscene, and no one should go to bed hungry or cold in a country that has so much to offer, so much money to spare.'' He shifted uncomfortably under her probing stare. "It's just as simple as that.''

She didn't answer for a moment as she rinsed off the dishes. Then she sat down at the table again. He might be trying to fool himself, but she wasn't buying it. What she saw was a man, a kind man with noble sentiments, who for some reason, couldn't open up. It was her guess that his work allowed him an avenue to do some real good without having to risk his innermost feelings. But nothing was ever gained without risk.

"No,'' she said thoughtfully, "I don't think it's simple, Starbuck. You say you don't like people, yet you're driven to help them—''

"I don't think *driven* is the right—''

"I do.''

"Doesn't anyone get to finish their sentences around you?'' he asked, with mounting exasperation.

His protest surprised her. She was just being helpful. "I knew what you were going to say.''

"Maybe you didn't.''

"All right.'' She folded her hands in her lap like an obedient child and looked up patiently. "Finish your sentence. You weren't going to say that you didn't think *driven* was the right word.''

The words came through clenched teeth. "I was.''

"Then I was right.''

He rose, dropping his napkin on the table. There was no winning with this woman. "Thank you for dinner.''

"No need to thank me. It's your aunt's house and her food.''

And it's going to stay that way, he said to himself as he walked out of the kitchen.

"Ricky." Her son turned startling green eyes in her direction from beneath the table. She scooped him up and set him back on his chair. But she was thinking about Justin. He seemed to be trying to communicate things to her through his kiss that he seemed unaware of on a conscious level. "He needs help."

"Help?"

"Yes, help." She stroked Ricky's silken hair slowly as she looked off in the direction in which Justin had gone. "I think Mr. Justin Starbuck desperately needs to be turned around. There's a good man inside there, locked up in a three-piece suit. And we—" she looked down at Ricky "—are going to be the ones to do it."

Down the hall, Justin shivered. He remembered the old superstition about someone having just stepped on his grave. He glanced back at the kitchen then picked up his pace.

Chapter Seven

It was the phone call heard around the world, or at least throughout the country, Philadelphia mused the following day. When they had returned from the hospital, she had called a local television station. Word of Rosalind's illness made the eleven o'clock news. By eight this morning, flowers, phone calls and telegrams came pouring in from everywhere.

"I will *never* get any work done," Angie moaned, opening the door as a delivery man appeared with yet another arrangement of white roses, Rosalind's favorite. "I might as well just stand here by the door all day."

"Here, I'll bring them to her," Philadelphia offered, taking the flowers from the man. "And that's not a bad idea," she commented to Angie. "You might save a few steps."

"And who'll make lunch?"

Philadelphia started up the stairs. "Good point. I'll send Margarita down."

"Ah!" Angie threw up her arms as the doorbell rang again. "I should have given my notice years ago."

She wasn't fooling Philadelphia. Angie was as happy about what was going on as she was. Rosalind needed this.

Her arms filled with roses, Philadelphia used her shoulder to push open Rosalind's door. "Delivery lady," she sang out. "Not, of course, that you need any more." Flower arrangements were vying for space in every available corner of the room.

"I *always* need more." Rosalind held her arms out for the latest arrivals.

Margarita had just finished arranging gladiolus in a cut-glass vase. "I have nothing left to put them in," she groaned, looking at the long-stemmed roses.

"Then send out for more vases," Rosalind instructed with a wave of her hand. "I'd forgotten how loved I was." With pleasure in her eyes, Rosalind surveyed the profusion of flowers.

It looked as if a florist's shop had exploded within the room. "No, you didn't," Philadelphia said affectionately.

"How did you get to know me so well in such a short time, girl?"

"I'm just naturally intuitive, I guess."

Rosalind laughed aloud for the first time in twenty-four hours. Philadelphia was grateful that she hadn't given in to Justin's scowl and not asked to have Rosalind released for a few days.

No one seeing her now would have guessed she needed surgery. She looked like a vibrant queen, not a triple-bypass candidate. Wearing a peignoir made of yards of blazing-red nylon, Rosalind sat on top of her bedspread, as always, propped up by a dozen pillows. The queen holding court, Philadelphia thought with a grin.

Philadelphia's attention was drawn to the astrology books that were scattered on the red-and-white velvet bedspread. A few lay opened, marked for further reading. She picked one up and glanced at it, then put it down.

"Seeing if next Saturday is a good day for surgery?" she asked. Margarita took the roses from Rosalind and went in search of vases, murmuring in Spanish under her breath.

Rosalind looked up from the telegram she was reading. There was a stack of them on the nightstand. She moved her reading glasses down her nose. "As a matter of fact, it is, but that's not what I'm looking into." She indicated the edge of her bed. "Sit."

"Yes, ma'am." Philadelphia didn't bother hiding her grin. "Oh, Margarita," she called to the departing maid, "Angie asked if you would go downstairs and take over answering the door."

"Mallory do it," Margarita announced, walking off with new determination.

"Do what?" Mallory asked, coming into the room. Three more telegrams were in his hand.

"Don't stand there with your mouth open, man. Bring those here." Rosalind stretched her hand out impatiently. There was obvious glee in her eyes.

It never hurt to know that you mean something to someone, Philadelphia thought. Abruptly, her thoughts turned to Justin. Did he mean anything to anyone besides Rosalind? Was there someone waiting for him at home? Someone he had made a commitment to? She doubted it. Rosalind would have mentioned that. From what she had said, his world was the Foundation. That left little time for a private life.

"Take Angie's place answering the front door," Rosalind added as an afterthought, tearing open the first of the telegrams he handed her. She pushed her glasses back into place.

Mallory shook his head. "What? And deprive that woman of something to complain about? That'll be the day." He watched Rosalind's face as she read. "Three more telegrams. Beats me how they found out about you being sick."

"People talk," Philadelphia said easily.

"Some people more than others."

The sound of his voice made her pulse jump. She turned slightly to see Justin walking into the room.

He fingered the top leaf of a giant potted dieffenbachia that had been sent by a former president. "Any more plants and flowers and this room is going to look like a jungle." He crossed the room and bent over Rosalind, kissing the smooth cheek. "So, how are you this morning, besides buried alive in flowers?" He took a step back to see for himself.

The deathly pallor that had worried him so much was gone. In part it was the makeup. The rest was spirit. Philadelphia had been right, he thought grudgingly.

"I feel wonderful. Ethan Thomas called this morning and wants to conduct a radio interview with me over the telephone." Enthusiasm made her look years younger than the woman who had been taken to the hospital just the morning before. "Frankly, I have to admit that I think the doctor is overdramatizing the situation."

An amused expression crossed Justin's face. "The *doctor* is overdramatizing?"

Rosalind put one hand to her breast, paused, then asked in studied astonishment, "Surely you don't mean to suggest that I overdramatize things?"

"I never said that." Justin noticed that Philadelphia was smiling to herself and wondered what she was thinking.

"See that you don't." Rosalind sighed, and Justin could almost see the screen persona receding for a moment. "I really don't think I need this operation."

Justin took her hand and looked at her kindly. Again, Philadelphia thought he seemed like another person when he was around his aunt, warm and caring and not at all afraid to let someone in. Which was the real Justin? She knew who she'd choose if she had a vote.

"The tests indicate that you do," Justin reminded her.

She turned her head toward Philadelphia. "And who interpreted the tests?"

"The doctor," Philadelphia volunteered. It earned her an annoyed look from Justin. "Well, he did."

"Exactly my point." Rosalind pulled her hand away from Justin to gesticulate. "The man probably needs a new car or something and wishes to use my heart as a means to get it."

"No one could ever be accused of using your heart, Aunt Roz."

"Trying, perhaps. But not succeeding." A satisfied smile lifted the corners of her ruby mouth. Arranging the folds of the shimmery peignoir, Rosalind looked from one face to the other. "I suppose I have no choice."

"No," Justin said firmly.

"Yes."

Justin's head whirled in Philadelphia's direction. He had purposely kept the length of the bed between them, but now he had an urge to leap over it and drag her away before she did any more damage. "Yes?" he echoed incredulously.

"Sure." Philadelphia addressed herself to Rosalind. After all, it was her health she was concerned with. Changing Justin's temperament was just going to have to wait. "It's very simple. You can go in and have the operation. Or you can stay here and die. The choice is still yours."

Rosalind frowned and looked at Justin. "She does have a way with words."

Justin picked up the closest telegram and scanned it, not seeing a single word. "I hadn't noticed."

Rosalind leaned back a little for a clearer view. "Oh, I think you have."

Even if this were a subject for discussion, which it wasn't, he didn't want it discussed in front of Philadelphia. Especially since he had lain awake half the night haunted by the effects of her mouth, both silent and otherwise.

He let the telegram fall onto the bed. "Well, I have work to do. Just came in to see how you're doing." He stopped and looked at all the opened books on her bed and the pad with pages of her scribblings on it. "*What* are you doing?"

"Plotting charts."

Philadelphia thought she detected something deliciously mischievous in Rosalind's voice.

Justin looked one book over and shook his head. He handed it back to Rosalind. "You mean as in navigation?"

"Something like that."

Rosalind shifted, struggling to sit up higher. Justin was quick to take her arm and add another pillow behind her back. Philadelphia was just as quick to add a small one on her other side. Their hands touched beneath the pillows. He pulled his back too quickly. He could see the amused look in Philadelphia's eyes. He swore under his breath.

The subject of their concern seemed oblivious to the by-play as she blissfully went on. "I'm doing a chart on the compatibility of a Capricorn and an Aries."

Justin stared at Rosalind, appalled. Philadelphia's hands flew to her mouth, covering it. In distress, he thought. Then a closer look at her eyes told him that the mouth behind those long, slender fingers was laughing.

Rosalind leaned over and extracted one volume from the heap. She tapped the third paragraph. "You might be interested in knowing, Justin, that the signs are very compatible," she said, a satisfied smile on her lips, "given the right moons."

Her eyes were twinkling at him. She was enjoying this. Enjoying watching him being uncomfortable.

He turned from Philadelphia and looked at his aunt. "No, I wouldn't be."

"Wouldn't be?" Rosalind echoed, her mind already busy with wedding arrangements. Justin's moon, she knew, was in Aquarius and that made all the difference, no matter how hard he fought against it. "Wouldn't be what, dear?"

"Interested, Aunt Roz." It was time for him to make an exit. He narrowly sidestepped Mallory, who was bringing in yet another huge potted plant. Helping the man, Justin took hold of the bottom and together they set the fern in the corner. "See you at lunch, Aunt Roz." He presented her with the card that was attached to the gift and left.

Rosalind shook her head, then patted her head to make sure no hair was out of place. "Stubborn. Even as a boy. Oh, how nice." The eyes crinkled as she read the card. "Lily Addams says she'll be praying for me. Well, that certainly can't hurt. If she doesn't have any pull up there, no one does. She used to be late to makeup every morning when we were doing *And One for Me.* Always went to church, first thing in the morning. Still does, I hear." Rosalind sighed, remembering better days.

Philadelphia drew closer on the huge bed, not wanting to interrupt but irresistibly curious. "What was he like as a boy?"

"Justin?"

Philadelphia nodded.

"Very lonely."

"An only child?" Philadelphia guessed.

Rosalind looked at Philadelphia's eyes, and a smile emerged as she obviously saw what she wanted to find. Her voice became subtly dramatic, reeling Philadelphia's emotions in. "Yes, but it was more than that. He was just excess baggage. Unwanted."

"Oh." The phrase Rosalind used crystallized a lot of things for Philadelphia. A pervading sadness flooded through her as she imagined how lonely Justin must have been. She thought of Ricky and what life might have been like if she had listened to Mark and put him up for adoption. Love helped overcome a lot of things. The lack of it could be devastating.

Rosalind moved her shoulders, inching herself higher against the pillows. The expression on Philadelphia's face was gratifying. Aries, once moved, threw themselves into things with enthusiasm. That included love. Rosalind hoped Justin was ready.

"I met Justin the summer I married his Uncle Alfred."

Philadelphia saw that Rosalind's eyes grew soft and misty as she said the older man's name. So, she had had a great love in her life. The thought pleased Philadelphia. "You miss him."

Rosalind was not ashamed to show her tender side. It was not something she did often, but there was an aura about Philadelphia that made Rosalind inherently trust the woman.

"Yes." Rosalind reached for Alfred's framed photograph on the nightstand. For a moment, she looked at it intently. "After all these years, I still do. He was a wonderful man who should have married me sooner." The words were filled with regret. "It would have given us more time together. Anyway..." She cleared her throat, dismissing the sentimentality. She had work to do, she thought, glancing at Philadelphia. But not too much as far as Philadelphia was concerned. "Alfred's brother, Arthur, was getting married and leaving on his honeymoon. He was going to leave his son alone with the servants while he was gone. From what I gather, since this was his third marriage, this wasn't the first time he had gone off and left Justin. I thought it was awful and told Alfred so. Justin was only eight at the time. I more or less grew up on my own and I knew how alone you can feel. I made Alfred fetch him here."

Rosalind shook her head and laughed, this time forgetting about the effect on her hairdo. "He was the sorriest excuse for a boy I had ever seen. More like a little old man, really. So solemn. Skinny, sad-eyed. His mother was dead, and his father had done a terrible job of raising him. Or—" she leaned forward to emphasize her point "—he had done a marvelous job of neglecting him, depending on how you viewed it."

She snorted when she thought of Arthur. There had never been any love lost there. "That man was so eager to find a sweet young thing to warm his bed that he completely ignored the love he had right in the palm of his hand." She closed her own hand and shook it in front of Philadelphia. "Justin wanted so badly to be loved by that pompous windbag."

Philadelphia saw anger in Rosalind's eyes. The violet became a dark shade of purple. She didn't envy Arthur any.

"I could have choked him with my bare hands. But I could never make him see. So, I did the next best thing. I took Justin over whenever I could. And there were plenty of opportunities. His father kept getting married and divorced, looking for the perfect mate. Justin stayed with me every summer and during every honeymoon. After a while, this was his home."

"He lived here?" Philadelphia asked. Justin hadn't mentioned that, but then, there was a lot Justin hadn't mentioned.

"Yes. The room he's in was his old bedroom."

That explained the decor, Philadelphia thought. Formal. Strong. It wasn't in keeping with the rest of the house.

"So, what do you think of him?"

Philadelphia raised her eyebrows. The woman certainly didn't pussyfoot. "You mean do I like him?" The sound of footsteps had her turning, but it was only Mallory with yet another delivery. This time, someone had sent flowers and candy. Rosalind held her hands out for the latter.

"Of course, I mean do you like him. What else would I mean? Philadelphia!" She protested as Philadelphia neatly intercepted the candy.

"Bad for your heart, remember?"

"Just one?"

"There is no such thing as just one piece of candy. You know that. Mallory, give this to Angie. Maybe it'll sweeten her up."

Mallory looked at Rosalind, and the woman finally nodded grudgingly. "Maybe I'm making a mistake, matching you up with Justin."

"Justin would certainly think so."

"What about you?"

Philadelphia shrugged. "What I think doesn't matter."

"It does to me."

Her words surprised Philadelphia. The lady had always done what she wanted to do, damn the consequences.

"Do you like him?" Rosalind pouted slightly as she watched Mallory retreat with the red box.

"Yes, I like him." She was attracted to Justin. *Really* attracted to him. She hadn't felt anything like this in a long, long time.

The man thinks you're an A1 pain in the neck. Leave it alone, Philadelphia.

Philadelphia's admission was exactly what Rosalind wanted to hear. She clapped her hands together. "Wonderful."

The scent from all the flowers was getting to the former star. Philadelphia rose and opened the window slightly. "You need a little air in here," she murmured, then turned from the window and looked at Rosalind. "I don't think you should clap just yet."

Rosalind swung her legs off the bed. She was damned tired of being tired. "Why not?"

Philadelphia watched her warily, afraid that the woman might fall if she tried to walk. But she knew better than to say that to Rosalind. "Because the feeling doesn't seem to be mutual." To her relief, Rosalind remained where she sat.

"Nonsense."

"Is that a direct order?" She leaned against the window seat, enjoying the fresh air that was coming in.

"No, that's a direct observation."

There were times it paid to be realistic, much as Philadelphia didn't care for it. "Seen through a lot of medication."

Rosalind shook her head. "I know that boy, Philadelphia. I know exactly what he needs." She tapped the book she had referred to previously. "They know, too."

"They?"

"The stars."

"I see." To laugh the way she wanted to would have been dangerous right now, Philadelphia told herself.

"Maybe not," Rosalind conceded shrewdly, "but you will."

"Yes, ma'am."

"Capricorns' passions are more controlled than the ones Aries are blessed with," Rosalind informed her, "but that doesn't mean they don't run deep. Once stirred, they're very loyal. It just takes a bit of work to get them there. I promise you, the tensions and misunderstandings you two might face seem formidable, but the rewards are tremendous. This is a happily-ever-after love we're talking about.''

"We'll see." Philadelphia thought of the papers in the den that she hadn't touched since Friday. "Well, I'd better get to work on your notes."

"Don't work too hard, Philadelphia," Rosalind cautioned just as Philadelphia crossed the threshold.

"Meaning take frequent breaks?"

"You're a bright girl."

"Yes, ma'am." She winked.

"And send Justin to me. Oh, and one more thing."

Philadelphia stopped, waiting. "Yes?"

"I'd like to thank you for releasing the story to the press."

She should have known Rosalind would figure it out. "Me?"

"You wouldn't have made it as an actress, Philadelphia."

"Yes, ma'am." Philadelphia laughed as she left.

She made her way down the hall and stopped by Justin's door. For once, she didn't hear him talking on the telephone. She raised her hand to knock, then stopped. What had these halls been like when he'd run up and down them as a child? *Had* he ever run up and down the halls? Were all the joys of being young taken away from him? No, not all. He might not have had a father's love, or a mother's, but he had had Rosalind, and a lot of people had had to make do on less.

Pushing her thoughts aside, Philadelphia knocked on the door, then peeked in.

Even without turning around, he knew it was her. She seemed to telegraph her presence to him. He didn't want to explore what that meant. He pushed his paper aside and looked up. "Don't you wait to be told to come in?"

She leaned against the door. "I thought if you knew it was me you might not tender the invitation."

"Wise guess." *Yes, I would have asked you in. I would have even shut the door. That's the problem.*

"Phone out of order?" She nodded toward it.

He had stood in his aunt's room and not consciously detected a single bloom. Philadelphia had entered the room, and suddenly he was surrounded by the scent of wildflowers. "No, why?"

"I didn't hear it ring."

He was struggling for composure. Having her here like this was a threat to his closely-guarded self. "Did you come in to check the phone line?"

She wondered if what had happened between them in the hall had been a mere matter of circumstances being just right. If so, how could she recreate those exact circumstances? "No, to tell you that your presence is requested."

"Since when do you issue formal—"

"I don't." She knew what he thought. "I barge in."

"I noticed."

"But your aunt would like to see you."

He looked at her quizzically. "She just—"

Philadelphia laughed. "She wants to 'just' again."

He pushed back his chair from the desk and studied her. "You know, between the two of you, I might forget how to form a complete thought."

Justin rose to his feet, careful not to move too close to her. He had gotten too close once, and disaster had struck. He wasn't up to round two. She'd win again. Odd, he thought of it as her winning. He was not much of a male conqueror, he reflected. But then, conquests had never interested him. He saw no satisfaction in knowing that if he came together with someone, eventually, inevitably, he would part from her.

"It'll come back to you," Philadelphia assured him, sauntering off.

He curbed an urge to follow her. Instead, he turned in the opposite direction and walked into his aunt's room. "You wanted me, Aunt Roz?"

"Yes. Come sit by me." She patted a space next to her.

"Oh-oh." Justin laughed as Rosalind raised an eyebrow. "Every time you call me over in that tone of voice, you usually want me to do something I don't want to." He grew serious then. "I'm not calling the doctor to cancel your surgery."

"No, nothing like that. I know I need it." For a moment, she looked close to her own age, but then she brightened. "If he does a good job, I can go on with my life just as I have."

Relief at her attitude was evident in his voice. "Telling people what to do."

Rosalind clamped her hand down on his. "Exactly."

"And what is it you want me to do?"

She didn't answer his question directly. Instead, she picked up the pages she had been working on. With careful fingers, she arranged them in a neat pile, then offered them to Justin. He took them from her and set them aside on the chair. Rosalind frowned. "I've always trusted the stars, Justin. I know you think it's a lot of nonsense—"

"Not nonsense exactly," he began tactfully.

"Then you do agree with them." More than a trace of hope was in her eyes.

"I didn't say that, either."

"Well—" she shrugged carelessly "—you needn't agree with them for them to be right."

"Fine, then there are no hurt feelings on their part."

"Don't be irreverent, Justin. The stars don't like being taken lightly. I've been doing a lot of reading—"

"You shouldn't tire yourself out." If it were up to him, he'd toss all of her books out. It was the one thing they had always disagreed on. Time and again, Rosalind would point out his traits in a book, trying to persuade him of the validity of her beliefs that people were guided by the stars. And time and again, he had bitten back the reply that given enough vague insinuations, *something* had to ring true, and it was the individual, not some seer of the stars, who interpreted things to mean what they did.

Rosalind held on to her books like a shield. "I don't know how much time I have," she admitted in a moment of utter honesty. "And I wanted to be sure."

He hated when she talked like that. It was so different from her usual, bombastic convictions that she would go on indefinitely. "You have forever. And be sure of what?"

"Of you and Philadelphia."

He wasn't exactly certain what she was driving at, but he had a nagging suspicion. Rising, he walked away from Rosalind. He crossed to the window and closed it. It was getting too cool. "I don't know about her, but you can be sure of me. I'll always stand by you."

"That's not what I mean."

"I was afraid of that."

Rosalind laid a hand reverently on top of one of her books. "She's a perfect match for you, Justin."

Humoring her was beyond his power. "I don't want a match, Aunt Rosalind, perfect or otherwise."

She became more serious. "You may not have something to say about it. This might well be a fated encounter, Justin, destined before either of you were born. Destined before time. It's written in the stars."

"As long as it's not carved in stone, it can be erased."

"Don't be flippant."

"Aunt Roz, I came to see you and to hold your hand through this operation. I did not come here for you to play matchmaker. What's come over you? You've never been concerned about seeing me matched before."

"I've never met anyone I ever thought was good enough for you before."

"And I have nothing to say about this?"

"Of course you do. You can say yes."

She watched as he crossed back to her. With a patient smile, Justin cleared away some of the books on her bed, stacking them on the chaise lounge. "What are you doing?"

"Clearing off a place for you. You need your rest." With gentle hands, he pressed her back until she was lying down again. "Your mind is working overtime."

She touched his hair, pushing back a wayward strand from his forehead. "I want to see you with someone, Justin. You need someone if anything should happen to me."

"I'm not that skinny little boy who walked into your parlor, Aunt Roz. And nothing is going to happen to you. I promise."

"You don't know that."

"I know that better than those stars of yours." He kissed the top of her head. "Now get some rest before I call Mallory in to stand guard over you."

"If you must call someone, get someone younger." A mischievous twinkle danced in her eyes.

He laughed. "I don't know anyone young enough for you." He slipped quietly out of her room. He had no idea why, but he was beginning to understand what a condemned man felt like.

Chapter Eight

"Bless you." Philadelphia handed Ricky a tissue and watched him wipe his nose haphazardly. "It's all in the wrist, my lad."

Taking the tissue from him, she made him blow, then tucked the covers around him. He looked particularly small in his bed tonight. Her thoughts were drawn to another little boy who probably had had no one to tuck him into bed at night, or care what time he was in bed.

"Don't wanna sleep," Ricky protested. The cold had him unusually cranky.

"Careful, you might grow up to be a grumpy old man, like someone else we know." She grinned as she thought of Justin. He had been deliberately avoiding her in the last twenty-four hours, ever since Rosalind's announcement that Capricorns and Aries were compatible. Just what was it he expected her to do, throw a net over him and dash off to a justice of the peace? That was definitely not her style. Friendly persuasion was more like it—if she thought he was worth the trouble. And she hadn't quite made up her mind that he was.

Ricky pushed away the covers. Just as firmly, Philadelphia tucked them around him again. "It gets chilly at night, young man. Here's Mr. Tiger."

Philadelphia placed the raggedy, limp tiger under his arm. The head wobbled from side to side. Ricky began to settle down a little. The hapless tiger always had a calming effect on him. He had had the toy since he was six months old. Now the faded tiger was splitting in several places, even though she had sewn every seam at least twice. His once-round little body now looked like the aftermath of a diet campaign. And the fragrance that lingered on the faded material was not the most pleasant. But Ricky loved him. Philadelphia had bought Ricky a new Mr. Tiger in hopes of throwing the old one away, but her son refused to part with his friend. He remained true to the wreck of a toy that had given up its stuffing in countless spins in the washing machine.

His little fingers tightened around the scrawny tiger. "You're loyal, I'll give you that." She sifted his hair through her fingers. Philadelphia frowned. His forehead felt warm. She hoped it would pass. She didn't need to worry about him as well as Rosalind. One problem at a time. "Hold on until after Saturday, okay?" she murmured.

"Sing, Momma."

"If I sing, will you go to sleep?"

"Yes!"

She laughed, gathering the small body to her and hugging him. "How come I don't believe you?"

Ricky's little shoulders moved up and down beneath his pajamas in an exaggerated shrug. "Dunno."

"My goodness, here less than three weeks and you're picking up her mannerisms already. We'll have you and

Rosalind doing scenes from Shakespeare before the year's out." The round face looked at her, bewildered. "Okay, okay. 'Momma sing.'" She mimicked his voice.

"Hold." He stuck out his free hand and waited until she took it.

"'Sing.' 'Hold.' Getting to be a regular little man-in-training, aren't you, my boy? Well, I don't respond to commands very well. Where's the magic word?"

"P'ease, Momma?"

"You got it."

Winding her fingers through his, Philadelphia settled into the roomy chair next to the youth bed and sang the lullaby that Ricky always wanted to hear. Over and over, she sang the familiar words until his eyes finally closed.

Her voice carried through the partially opened door, drifting into the hallway. Justin stopped. He had been on his way downstairs to the kitchen, but her voice made him forget why.

She had a haunting voice. He tried to shut it out as he began to cross the stairs. He got no farther than her door. A moment wouldn't cost him, he thought, pausing.

A moment fed into a minute, a minute into five. The words of her song were simple, a mother's love for a child. Yet somehow they spoke to him, wakening an ache he had long since thought had vanished. He had never known a mother's love, never felt a parent's affection. And though he had Roz and blessed the day his uncle had met her, it wasn't the same. The cold, hard fact was that he had been rejected, had been the child neither parent had taken the time to love.

Damn her for reminding him of it. Damn her for reminding him that though he tried to deny them, there were needs within him. The same needs that had brought his father to emotional ruin.

As he listened, the tune that had brought him sadness brought him peace. It soothed, like soft, tapering fingers kneading away the pain.

He envied her son, just as he had envied so many others as he was growing up. Ricky would never lack for a mother's love, never wonder what it was about him that made him so unlovable. Justin acknowledged Rosalind had made him whole again, rebuilt his confidence, but even she could never erase that initial doubt. With all his money, he was poorer than Ricky. Philadelphia would never let Ricky suffer a moment of self-doubt. If the last day was any indication of the way she lived her life, she'd keep Ricky's days and nights too full to leave him any time to wonder why his father walked out and if he was the cause.

Justin roused himself. He couldn't just stand here in the hallway, sprouting roots into the carpet. If she came out now and saw him—

She did come out.

"Oh." She looked up in surprise, startled to see him there. Behind her, she eased the door closed softly. "Hello." Memories of their last time alone together in the hallway taunted her. She wondered what the chances were of déjà vu.

He cleared his throat. "You have a very nice voice."

"Ricky likes it." She shrugged off his compliment, though it pleased her. "I wish Ricky liked more than one song, though, but he seems to be a creature of habit. Like that stuffed animal of his. It should have been thrown out a long time ago, but he just won't let go of it."

A muted image, blunted by time, flashed through Justin's mind. A rabbit whose head was only half on. He had been extra careful not to let the tear go any farther. But eventually it had. One of his governesses had thrown the rabbit away, then chided him when he had cried. It was the last time he had displayed emotion. "I had a stuffed animal like that once."

"You?"

"Yes, me." He saw the incredulous look in her eyes. He knew he was going to hate himself for asking. "What's the matter?"

"I can't picture you attached to anything like that." She thought of the man who had kissed her with passion, passion that had probably surprised him more than her. "On second thought, maybe I can at that."

Justin knew better than to ask her what she meant. "That song you were singing, I've never heard it before."

"That's probably because I made it up."

"You write music?" The woman probably mastered everything in her spare time. She struck him as an overachiever. Disorganized but pushy.

"No, not really. It just came, that's all. I—uh-uh." She looked up as the hall lights flickered overhead. "Looks like we might—" The lights went out. "—Lose power."

Suddenly, they were engulfed in darkness. Instinctively, she took a step closer to Justin, drawn by the heat of his body. She reached out and placed her hand on his arm. He tensed under her touch. "Just getting my bearings, Starbuck." *Don't panic, I won't attack you,* she added silently. "Thank goodness Ricky fell asleep," she murmured. "He hates the dark."

"Can't say I'm too fond of not seeing where I'm going myself," Justin commented. She slid her hand down his arm and took his hand. He shuddered and was grateful for the dark.

"Here, hold on to me."

"Don't tell me, let me guess. You can see in the dark like a cat." He had always thought she had the eyes for it.

"No, but if I hold on to you, we won't trip over each other as we make our way to the stairs, will we?" Slowly, she felt along the wall and moved forward.

The thought of their bodies touching was not as repugnant to him as she made it sound. "That remains to be seen." She tugged on his hand to keep him moving. He grimaced. "Shouldn't I be leading?"

"Why? Are we dancing?"

Her hand touched the outline of a door. She pushed, and it opened. It was his room. Moonlight shone through the window. She left the door open, taking advantage of the scant light.

"No, but I am the man here." He felt her turn. Her hair brushed along his chin, creating an exceptionally erotic response. His body tightened. Yes, he was the man here, all right.

"Was that being questioned?" she asked innocently.

He could *feel* her smile. "Philadelphia, have you always been this maddeningly independent?"

"I think so. Do you know that that's the first time you've said my name in the context of a sentence?" She began moving again.

"I wasn't keeping score." Failing to move when she did, he almost tripped when she pulled.

"Careful."

"I think I'll do better if you stop dragging me." He let go of her hand.

"I wasn't aware that I was." There was a thud, then the sound of something tottering. He had probably walked into the small table that stood against the wall between the two rooms. *Good, serves you right,* Philadelphia thought.

He rubbed his leg. "I heard that."

"Heard what?"

"That stifled laugh."

"Sorry."

"No, you're not."

"Have it your way."

His laugh was short. "Not with you around."

"Philadelphia, are you out there? What's going on?" They had reached Rosalind's door. Rosalind didn't sound distressed so much as annoyed at the inconvenience the blackout caused.

Philadelphia skimmed her hand along the wall, looking for the door. Rough material met the tips of her fingers. Justin's chest. "Sorry," she murmured to him. "Nothing much," was the answer she gave Rosalind.

That was her opinion, Justin thought. Her groping touch had made him want to complete something that had been started yesterday.

"See what you can do about this, girl," Rosalind instructed.

"Will do."

"Philadelphia declared 'let there be light.' And it was good," Justin said sarcastically.

Ever so slowly, she resumed feeling her way toward the stairs. "Misquoting the Bible, Starbuck?"

"Writing new chapter and verse, according to you."

"If we're going to fight, can we do it with the lights on?" She wondered what was it about her that kept setting him off. What sort of women was he used to, shrinking violets who sat in ivory towers, waiting to have everything done for them? That wasn't her way, and he had darn well better get used to it.

"Is that you, Justin?" Rosalind's voice floated into the hall.

Justin paused, then turned his head so his voice carried. "Yes, Aunt Roz."

"Oh, good."

"Want me to stay with you?" he offered.

"No, carry on."

He heard the woman chuckling to herself. "She probably thinks 'the stars' fooled around with the electrical system just to trap us in the dark," he muttered.

Philadelphia laughed. He wished she wouldn't. Her laugh was low and silky. As illogical as it seemed, the mere sound of her laugh created urgent desires within him.

It was all physical, he told himself. And yet, he knew that the pull he was feeling was not entirely so basic. Something more was going on, something that could lead to his undoing.

A flicker of light came their way. Angie, hefting two flashlights and pointing a third, with Margarita in her wake, was walking toward them. "I think it's the darn circuit breaker again," she grumbled.

"Does this happen often?" Philadelphia asked.

"Often enough," Angie complained. "Last time was about three years ago."

Anything, apparently, was an inconvenience to Angie. "May I have one of those?" Philadelphia asked, nodding toward the flashlight. "I'll go out and throw the switches."

Angie handed Philadelphia the flashlight. Justin looked on, wondering if Philadelphia was doing this on purpose or if she was so used to having to do things for herself that it never crossed her mind to turn to him. It also occurred to him that he *wanted* her to need his help. That annoyed him, but there was no denying the fact. He felt like a teenager again, wanting to flex his muscles for a girl on the beach. Except there was one thing wrong. As a teenager, he had never wanted to flex his muscles for a girl on the beach. Maybe this was just a delayed reaction. Fifteen years delayed.

"I take it you're not waiting for a knight in shining armor to come riding up."

"Why?" Philadelphia asked innocently. "Are you volunteering?"

"No," he bit off.

"Then it's a good thing I'm not waiting, isn't it?"

Angie looked at them and shook her head, disgusted. "I'll let you two argue this out. I'm going in to Rosalind. Coming, Margarita?"

Margarita nodded, barely leaving any space between them as she hurried after the small woman casting a huddled, misshapen shadow on the wall. Margarita was afraid of the dark and not embarrassed about letting it be known.

Justin glanced down at the floor as Philadelphia pointed the flashlight ahead of them. Her feet were bare. "Don't you want to put shoes on, first?"

"No need to be formal," she answered with a grin. "I feel better in bare feet."

"Suit yourself."

"I usually do."

"So tell me, how long have you felt the need to bend steel in your bare hands?"

She stopped and turned around. With the light from the flashlight casting large silhouettes on the wall, she looked smaller than she was. Smaller and softer. "Since I've been on my own. Since I found out that not all promises are kept. And since," she added, her mouth softening into a smile, "I've gotten this overpowering urge to wear blue tights, put on a red cape and fly."

He couldn't help grinning. "That would explain it. Let's get on with it, Supergirl."

"Woman," she corrected pointedly. "Superwoman."

The beam cast an exaggeration of her curves on the wall as they went down the stairs. "Right. Woman," Justin murmured, wishing the fact wasn't so obviously evident.

Outside the house, with the moon drifting behind a cloud, visibility did not improve. Philadelphia stopped for a moment. "Looks kind of pretty, doesn't it?"

"If you like that sort of thing."

"Don't stop much to smell the roses, do you, Justin?"

Something rippled through him when she said his name. He was just getting used to her calling him Starbuck. "Right now, I can't even find the roses. Let's get this over with. Hand me the flashlight."

"Oui, mon capitaine." She thrust it at him abruptly.

He hadn't expected her to relinquish it so easily. The flashlight slipped out of his hand and fell to the ground, rolling under the hedge. "One word, Philadelphia, and it'll be your last."

"My lips are sealed," she said innocently.

"If only that could be true." With an impatient sigh, Justin knelt down, groping along the ground near the hedges. The flashlight had managed to shut itself off as it hit the ground. There was no telltale light to guide him. He turned and bumped into something soft. Too soft. Reaching over, he realized too late that she was beside him, trying to help.

This wasn't helping anything, he thought. He heard her sharp intake of breath and knew instantly just what it was he had touched. The tips of his fingers warmed even as he drew his hand away from her breast.

Philadelphia cleared her throat. "I don't think this is the kind of electricity that'll light up the house," she murmured, rocking back on her heels.

His urge to touch her again, to kiss her and feel her against him, soft, pliant, womanly, was almost overwhelming.

The trick to maintaining his sanity, he decided, was to get back among other people. Quickly. He felt along the ground away from her and his fingers locked around a cylindrical form. "I found it."

Philadelphia sensed him backing away from her. Did he really dislike her that much? No, it wasn't that. She was sure of it. "I think we found more than the flashlight, Justin."

He rose quickly to his feet, then extended his hand to her. "Do you know where the circuit breaker is?"

"Tactfully put." She took his hand. The firm, impersonal grip stung her. "I thought you lived here."

Justin worked hard to control his breathing. It annoyed him that she seemed to know a lot about him and he nothing of her. Except that he wanted her. "How did you know that?"

"Your aunt told me."

"Yes. I lived here for a while a few years ago."

Philadelphia raised his hand and turned the flashlight on, shining it along the far wall. "Then why don't you know where the circuit breaker is?"

He wondered if she was trying to make him feel like an idiot on purpose. No, he was doing too good a job of that himself. "There was never a need to know, all right?"

"All right," she echoed pleasantly, trying her best not to show him his withdrawal had hurt her. "It's over here."

Her knowing that annoyed him even more. "How do you know that?"

"I like to know my way around." She couldn't resist adding, "We Aries are like that." She raised his hand higher. She saw the look that came over his face. "Just directing you. Nothing personal, Starbuck. Shine it over here.''

Justin gritted his teeth. So he was Starbuck again and they were back in their corners. Better that way, he thought. So why did it irritate him? Because *she* irritated him with every breath she took. Every breath that moved her firm breasts up and down, every breath that passed through her warm, inviting body.

Swearing softly, he moved after her. She heard him, but made no comment. Philadelphia threw the switches one by one.

Justin looked up at the mansion. It was still dark. "All right, Mr. Wizard, now what?"

She sighed. If he was deliberately trying to provoke her, he was going to be disappointed. "Now we find candles," she said with forced cheerfulness. She was going to stay cheerful if it killed her.

She moved to the side and looked out toward the front of the house. In the distance, she could usually see the house across the street. Tonight there were no lights evident. "The whole neighborhood's dark. We're having a power failure."

He glanced at her before he pointed the flashlight in the opposite direction. "I should be so lucky." He retraced his steps to the back door. For once, she followed him.

Silence always drove her crazy. "Have you had dinner yet?" she finally asked. The silence had lasted all of five seconds.

"No."

"Me, neither. Sandwiches all right?"

"Fine." He pushed open the door and held it for her. "I'll make them."

She walked in without sparing him a glance. "If that makes you feel better." She let her words sink in for a moment. "We can have them in the living room."

He sighed. Getting the last word was a losing battle, and winning didn't mean as much as it had. "Don't you ever get tired of giving directions?" He aimed the flashlight along the tiled floor, guiding them into the living room.

"Hasn't happened yet."

"Let me know when. I'd like to be there." He paused as they reached the room. "You'll be all right here?"

She softened at the note of concern in his voice. "It's been a long time since I've been afraid of the dark."

"Me," he said under his breath as he left, "I'm terrified." Especially of being in the dark with her.

Standing the flashlight on its end in the kitchen, he quickly fixed sandwiches, idly wondering how long it would be before Angie's precious food supply would spoil. He knew she'd have a few choice things to say about his opening the refrigerator. It seemed to him that the house was suddenly filled to overflowing with opinionated women. He and Mallory didn't stand a chance.

Impulsively, he put a bottle of wine and two long-stemmed glasses on the tray. As he placed the sandwiches next to them, Mallory peered in, obviously looking for Angie. Satisfied that she wasn't there, Mallory hurried over to the refrigerator and took out a can of beer from the back.

"Nothing I hate more than warm beer," Mallory pronounced. "This is a mercy drinking, you know."

Justin laughed. Mallory towered over Angie, yet the small woman held him on a leash. "Angie is upstairs with my aunt. Tell her that the problem was larger than Superwoman could handle. Seems we're having a power failure."

"Will do." Mallory nodded, downing the contents of the can. Carefully, he got rid of the evidence and made his way out. "Superwoman," he chuckled under his breath.

Tray in hand, flashlight carefully tucked under his arm, Justin made his way back to the living room.

Philadelphia had a fire going in the fireplace. He might have known she would. Forgetting his vow not to stay in the dark alone with her, Justin set the tray down on the coffee table.

She looked at the tall bottle and glasses on the tray. "Sandwiches and wine?" she observed. "That sounds too unorthodox for you, Starbuck."

"You can't pigeonhole me that easily."

"How easily can I pigeonhole you?" she asked, amused.

"Eat."

"Yes, master." She flopped down on the sofa and picked up a sandwich.

Awkward. He felt awkward again. He thought of sitting down in the easy chair, but knew it would look too obvious. She'd probably have something to say about it. She talked too much as it was.

He sat down next to her and immediately regretted it. Her knee brushed against his, and that was enough. His prodigious appetite suddenly had nothing to do with the sandwich that sat on the plate before him.

"This is kind of cozy," she commented.

Too much so. Justin decided that he had better leave while he still could. "I should see about Aunt—"

"I've already told her about the power failure."

Foiled again. "Isn't there anything you haven't taken care of?"

She lowered her sandwich, looking at him meaningfully. "I can think of one."

He didn't ask what it was.

She saw him withdrawing again. She wondered if it was her, then discarded that idea. It was him. And she was going to have to do something about that. "You're a very complicated man, Starbuck."

"Not really. I've always thought of myself as simple." Too late, he regretted his choice of words.

But for once she seemed serious. "You don't strike me as simple."

"Just what do I strike you as?" He knew he was digging his own grave.

"Someone who requires a lot of patience to get to know."

"I'm very busy."

"You're very defensive," she corrected.

"Of what?"

"Of your space."

He knew she was right there. But why did it sound so cold? "Let's just say I don't care for invaders."

She had never known how to waltz around words. Her way was to get right to the heart of the matter. "Is that what I am to you, an invader?"

She was crowding him again. His fears made him want to run.

"Philadelphia, let's get something straight. I've never seen a relationship that worked."

So that was it, she thought. "How many have you seen?"

He thought of all his father's marriages. Promising to love and cherish until death do they part, then parting within six months. "Enough."

"No, I'd say just the opposite is true."

Her mouth was close to his as she spoke. Too close. He saw the firelight play upon it.

And then he couldn't see her lips anymore. They were covered by his own.

Chapter Nine

There were at least a dozen reasons why he shouldn't be kissing her and only one reason why he should. Because he wanted to.

He was experienced enough to know that this was definitely something different, something more complicated than a simple sexual reaction. For one thing, he had never felt as if he was free-falling off a cliff when he kissed a woman before.

What was it about this headstrong, contrary woman that had made him come undone? In his everyday world, he functioned like a precision instrument. With her, he was like a blade that had gone dull.

Instrument. Hell, maybe that was the problem. Instruments didn't feel. And he felt. With her in his arms, he felt an entire spectrum of feelings. Weak, strong, light-headed, alert. Hungry. And he knew that feelings led to problems. Hadn't feelings led his father blindly into bad marriages? Hadn't feelings been what had allowed him to be hurt so badly as a child? Without feelings, he could see clearly, could accomplish things. What did it matter that the accomplishments didn't bring this kind of a surge with them? That didn't lessen his accomplishments. He had started and piloted a foundation that helped feed and clothe people who would otherwise do without, who would otherwise starve. That should be enough.

It wasn't.

Holding Philadelphia in his arms, running his hands along the curve of her back, kissing lips made that much more tempting by the soft glow from the fireplace, filled out the empty corners of his soul the way no antiseptic list of achievements ever possibly could.

He knew he should stop kissing her.

He didn't want to stop. In a minute, maybe, but for now, the folly was committed and he wanted to savor it just a little longer.

His hands tangled in her hair as his mouth slanted, taking, feeding, giving. Drawing life. A man could get lost in what he found here. Right now, that didn't seem like such a terrible option.

Philadelphia returned his kisses, feeling like a giddy child again, head spinning, senses reeling, hanging on for dear life as she plunged down in the first car of a roller coaster, taking hills and valleys at breakneck speeds. She hadn't felt like this since—

She had *never* felt like this.

She didn't want to stop feeling like this. Ever.

Her toes curled, but the rest of her opened up like a thirsty flower in the first drought-breaking rain. She clutched at the sleeves of the sweater he was wearing. For such a strait-laced person, he packed an incredible wallop. More incredible than that, he evoked hungers and passions from her that she had only been vaguely aware of. Though she gave freely of her affections, she had only been in love once before. And Mark had never made her feel like this. Her pulse had never threatened to leap out of her wrist. Her heart hadn't skipped beats, then pounded madly. And there was this funny rushing noise in her ears. She was drowning, and she was more than happy to go.

An involuntary groan escaped her lips when Justin drew back. "Remind me to send a thank-you note to the electric company," she murmured.

He didn't want to stop kissing her. He *had* to stop kissing her. Now. Justin knew he was tottering on the brink and he couldn't let himself go over. Or was it already too late?

The outline of her lips was slightly blurred from the force of his mouth on hers. Unable to help himself, he ran his hands through her hair. Touching her was as necessary at this moment as breathing. "I've never met anyone like you, Philadelphia."

"Is that good or bad?"

"The jury's still out on that."

"At least you're honest." She feathered her fingers along his face, liking the rough feel of his cheek. The first signs of a beard were starting. A five o'clock shadow. She wondered if he'd look more roguish in a beard, then decided it didn't matter *what* he looked like. It was what he was that mattered. "Although you certainly don't kiss as if you're undecided about me."

No, he thought, he didn't. Which worried him. This was happening much too fast for him, although she seemed to be taking it in stride.

How many others had she kissed like this? "You've had a lot of experience at this."

Her rosy glow died abruptly. Philadelphia backed away. Her eyes narrowed. "At what?"

He gestured helplessly, unable to phrase it. "This."

"Kissing?" Her tone was guarded. How could he? Just because she had loved a man once, the wrong man, how could he insinuate—

"That and..." Again, words failed him. He didn't want them spoken between them. He didn't want to know. And yet, something drove him on. He had to know.

This time, she waited for him to finish, but he didn't. She crossed her arms before her. "You're always complaining that I don't let you complete a sentence. Well, I'm waiting."

He didn't like the anger in her tone, and his temper rose, fueled by the fact that he had caused the hurt he saw in her eyes. "You know what I mean."

"I'm hoping I don't." Her temper flared. Was he really going to ruin it all by inferring something horrible? "Do you mean that you think I sleep around?"

"I didn't say that."

"No, but that's what you so ineloquently meant, isn't it?"

"I—"

"Well, I don't. Ricky is here because I loved his father. And if it is any business of yours, he was the only one I slept with." She nearly upset the coffee table as she got to her feet. There was going to be a bruise on her shin tomorrow, she thought. Maybe it would remind her not to be so quick in making decisions about people. "Now, if you'll excuse me..."

"Here," he called after her. When she turned, he raised the flashlight. "You might need this."

Damn, it wasn't what he wanted to say at all. But it was better to let her go angry than to let anything further develop.

She glared at the offering. "Don't tempt me. I just might use it on your head."

He should have let her go, but he couldn't. Not like this. Two strides and he was at her side. He found he had to exert a mild amount of force to turn her around. She might look small and petite, but she was stronger than he gave her credit for. And more stubborn than a human being had a right to be.

"Philadelphia, I'm sor—" He let out an angry breath and started again. "I'm sorr—"

Despite her anger, a smile found its way to her lips. Her temper was mercurial, and she was just as glad to bury it as she was to let it loose.

"Are you trying to apologize, or do you have a slow leak?"

He held her by the shoulders, almost at arm's length. It was as close as Justin trusted himself to be. "The former."

"Words really aren't your strong point, are they?"

"They were until two days ago."

He studied her face for a moment and wondered what there was that pulled at him so. She was a pretty girl, but that wasn't it. When analyzed, each part of her could be judged attractive, but it was a case of the whole thing being greater than the sum of its parts. Something about destiny crossed his mind, but he refused to explore it. That was his aunt's game, not his.

"I didn't mean to pry into your personal life, and I didn't mean to make it sound as if I thought that you, well, that you—"

"Apologies aren't your strong point, either," Philadelphia observed with a genial smile. "We'll drop it, all right?"

"All right." And then, because he couldn't let it lie, he changed his mind. "No, not all right."

It was her turn to be confused. It was a night for confusion, she decided. First he wanted her, then he acted as if he

didn't. One of them was going to have to make up his mind.
"What?"

"I want to ask you something."

"What?"

"Why did he leave you?"

"Mark?" Looking up into Justin's eyes, it was even hard
to remember the other's name. Or even that an other had
existed.

"Is that his name?" He had never liked the name Mark,
he decided.

"Yes, that's his name. That *was* his name." Philadelphia
looked off into the fire, trying to distance herself from the
final scene that had once hurt so much. "And he left because he didn't want to be poor."

"I don't understand." How could anyone having her love,
her child, ever think of himself as poor? The thoughts ran
through Justin like quicksilver and warned him that he was
on dangerous ground.

She sighed, remembering. "He came from a very promi-
nent family. His mother didn't think I was good enough for
her only son. She offered to buy me off. Literally. Looking
back, maybe I should have taken it. She was offering a lot
more than Mark was ultimately worth." Philadelphia ran
her hand through her hair the way she did when she was
trying to rid herself of something. "So she tried her hand at
threatening."

"She threatened you?" he asked incredulously.

"No, she threatened Mark with disinheritance. It was
amazing how fast he changed his mind about us once she did
that."

"And he left you?" He thought of the sleeping boy upstairs. "And Ricky? Just like that?"

"Ricky wasn't Ricky yet. I was pregnant when Mark
left."

"And he..."

"Never bothered to find out," she ended. "So I never bothered to tell him he had a son. As far as I'm concerned, Ricky's mine, not his." Her voice became quiet, distant. "Mark died in a plane crash last year. A private plane going to a jet-set party where he could mingle with people who had his mother's nod of approval."

He expected bitterness from her. Instead, he heard only sadness. That's all there was, sadness for a wasted life.

She turned from the fire, her features almost golden in the glow. "That's all in the past. I don't want to talk about Mark anymore."

Because he couldn't help himself, because she had moved him, Justin took a step closer to her. "Neither do I."

She was more than willing to meet him halfway. "What would you rather do?"

"Probably go down for the third time," Justin speculated before he allowed himself to kiss her again. And again. And again. His hands worked their way beneath her sweater, spanning her waist, molding her against him and his flaming desire. She felt so soft, so good. Hesitantly, he extended his fingers and lightly brushed them against her breasts. She shuddered, and her kiss grew more passionate in response.

The lamps flashed on all around them, and they sprang apart, eyes blinking to accustom themselves to the sudden burst of light.

"I guess the power failure's over," he said.

She caught the regret in his voice. What would have happened between them if the lights had never come on? She ached to know. "I guess it is."

It helped him to know that her breath was as ragged as his own. But it didn't alleviate the gnawing hunger. Justin hesitated for a moment, reluctant to let her go. Finally, though, he released her. "Well, I have work to do."

"Now?" She glanced down at her wristwatch, then stared at him.

"Now."

If he didn't get away from her, he was going to do something he knew he would regret. Although his resolve was weakening, he didn't believe in relationships, knew that they were all a dead end. And he didn't want to start one with her.

But he already had.

Philadelphia had little time to ponder Justin's behavior the next day. Rosalind, two days away from going in for her surgery, was making the most of her borrowed time. She had decided to throw herself into her memoirs with a vengeance, as if starting something like that would guarantee that she had to return home again to finish the project. In addition, because of Philadelphia's phone call to the TV station, the estate had become the site of a continuous parade of people coming and going. Friends, florists, interviewers, all came to pay their respects and wish her well. An endless stream of cards and telegrams kept arriving. Rosalind was in seventh heaven.

Thursday was one of the two days that Philadelphia dropped Ricky off at nursery school. She thought that the three-hour stint with other children his age was good for him. It also afforded her more time to work on Rosalind's book without being interrupted.

Used to functioning in the eye of a hurricane, Philadelphia still found it difficult to concentrate with the doorbell ringing and the constant babble of people's voices. Finally, giving up, she walked out of the den and stood in the doorway, looking up the stairs. A tall, distinguished man she vaguely recognized but couldn't place was just leaving Rosalind's bedroom. A heavyset woman was puffing as she grasped the railing and made her way slowly up the spiral staircase.

It had been like this for two days, beginning the day of the power failure and escalating. Philadelphia knew that Rosalind was in her glory, and it made Philadelphia feel warm that she had had a hand in getting it all rolling. She hoped all this would get Rosalind's mind off the actual surgery. Dwelling on it served no purpose. What had to be had to be.

It was something Rosalind might have said to her, quoting from one of her books, Philadelphia thought with a smile. In the last couple of days, she had learned more about her own astrological sign and Justin's than she cared to know. Rosalind had insisted Philadelphia read up on it and then pointedly asked her questions when Philadelphia entered her bedroom. Rosalind seemed more interested that Philadelphia grasp the facts about Justin's sign than in her making headway with the memoirs. Odd, Philadelphia mused.

She wondered if a deep, dark foreboding premonition was urging Rosalind to tie up all the loose ends and to see everyone she knew just once more. Philadelphia knew all the facts and figures about the operation. It was basically safe. Still, there was always that prospect of... She shuddered. She could only guess how Rosalind was handling that beneath her regal facade.

Suddenly wanting to look in on her, Philadelphia took advantage of the break in traffic to quickly hurry up the stairs. The heavyset woman had stopped her ascent, resting on the tenth step. The dapper old man winked at Philadelphia as he passed her.

Now why couldn't Justin be more open like that? Philadelphia wondered.

But then he wouldn't be Justin, she thought with a resigned sigh.

"Hi." Philadelphia peeked into Rosalind's room. She could hardly see her for all the flowers, and made her way carefully, forging a path between several potted plants. "Need anything?"

"Some of your energy would be nice." Rosalind carefully rearranged her bed jacket.

"Sorry, fresh out." Absently, Philadelphia smelled an arrangement of carnations that had been brought in that day. The card was still attached to the vase. She glanced at it. It bore the name of their local senator. "I could bring you coffee or something, though."

"Could you sneak up some brandy?"

Philadelphia raised an eyebrow. "Doctor said no spirits."

"The doctor *has* no spirit. Speaking of spirit—" a mischievous look entered her eyes "—do you know who you just passed in the hall?"

"He looked familiar, but—no." Philadelphia shook her head.

"That was Gabriel Saunders. My very first leading man." Rosalind sighed, rolling her eyes toward the ceiling. "When I think of how we used to burn up the celluloid—and several other things as well..." She pressed her lips together, lost for a moment in memories, then looked at Philadelphia. The pose evaporated, and the somber expression that suddenly appeared brought a flash of vulnerability to Rosalind's eyes. "I'm afraid, Philadelphia," she whispered.

Philadelphia sat down on the edge of the bed and took the woman's hand, squeezing it. "You wouldn't be human if you weren't, Rosalind. It's going to be all right, I promise." She held back a wave of tears that had suddenly formed. "God's not ready to have you take over heaven just yet."

A deep, pleased chuckle rose from within Rosalind's ample bosom. "No, I guess not." She moved her head slightly, trying to see who had entered the room. "Delia, how are you?"

Philadelphia turned to see that the short, round-faced woman had finally made it into the room. "I'd be better if you were on the first floor," the woman gasped.

"Why didn't you use the elevator, dear?" Rosalind purred sweetly.

Philadelphia got the distinct impression of two female cats waltzing around each other. This was good for Rosalind, she thought. Got her spirits fighting.

Not wanting to get in the way, Philadelphia rose. "Well, I'd better see about getting back to work—"

As she turned to leave, she saw Justin entering the room. "Philadelphia, you had a call."

No one called her here. She looked at him quizzically. "Did they say who it was?"

"Ricky's nursery school teacher." He saw concern leap into her eyes.

"What . . . ?"

"Ricky threw up all over the finger-paint jars. The woman says he's running a fever."

Philadelphia glanced over her shoulder toward Rosalind. A bejeweled hand waved her out. "Take that boy to the doctor, Philadelphia. Have Mallory drive you."

Philadelphia was already hurrying from the room. Justin kept pace. "I'll drive," he offered.

Philadelphia stopped momentarily to look at him. This wasn't like him. It was more in keeping with the man she only *hoped* he was. "Don't you have work to do?"

"Weren't you the one who told me I should get out among the less fortunate?"

She took the stairs quickly, telling herself that she was overreacting. Every little boy threw up and ran a fever. But this was *her* little boy. Somehow, that made it different. "I never thought of myself as less fortunate."

"Funny, I did."

She threw the front door open, then stopped, remembering that she had forgotten her purse. "You thought of me as less fortunate?"

"No, I used to think of myself that way. Other kids had a mother and father, I had servants."

Forcing herself to calm down, she let the full meaning behind Justin's words sink in. He was trying to help. It had a nice feeling to it. Maybe she wasn't wrong about him, after all. Or about them.

"I'm afraid that doesn't quite qualify you for a welfare dole, but maybe you're right, after all. You were less fortunate in that case. No time like the present to change that."

He held back an exasperated sigh. Now what the hell did she mean by that? He was afraid to ask. A lot of the things she said were best left unclarified—for both their sakes.

"Just let me get my purse." Without waiting for his answer, she dashed into the den. "The nursery school," Philadelphia called out, then crossed back to the hallway, "is just a mile away."

He wondered if she was capable of moving slowly, then remember the way her body had slowly moved against his. Sometimes, he thought. Sometimes. "Don't you have to call the doctor for an appointment?"

"It might be just a simple cold." Valiantly, she tried to convince herself that she was right.

"What if it's not?" he asked, opening the front door.

Philadelphia rolled her eyes. "*Then* I'll call the doctor."

He muttered something about her being too laid back and walked ahead of her to the garage.

Fifteen minutes later, when she called Ricky's pediatrician, Justin merely smiled his triumph.

"There's 'I told you so' written all over your face," she said, putting down the receiver. Ricky was cradled against her, his small body propped up in the crook of her other arm.

Justin had no idea that his sentiments were so obvious. People had always told him that his expression was unreadable. "You could have saved yourself some time if you had made the appointment earlier."

"Half an hour is not going to change the course of history, Justin." She shifted Ricky's weight, dividing it between both arms now. The boy was small, but he was growing heavier by the minute. "Tell your aunt I'll be back as soon as possible."

Ricky was burning up, and Philadelphia was annoyed with herself for having taken him to nursery school. But he had seemed fine this morning, eager to play with his friends. She was being overprotective, she told herself. With her purse hooked over one shoulder, she made her way to the door.

Justin was there ahead of her, opening it again. "Aunt Roz already told you to go to the doctor. I think she'll be able to figure out where we've gone."

Philadelphia glanced at him. "We?"

He closed the door behind them. "You need someone to drive, don't you?"

"I've been driving since I was sixteen. Besides, there's Mallory."

Justin wasn't going to argue with her, and he wasn't going to let her go alone. She was just being perverse, he decided, which, according to what his aunt kept telling him, was par for the course for an Aries. Maybe there was something to this star business, after all. At least as far as Philadelphia was concerned.

Ricky dropped his Mr. Tiger and whined. Justin picked it up and handed the mangy animal back to him, wrinkling his nose slightly. He had smelled better things in his time.

"Do you want to get that boy to a doctor or do you want to stand out here and argue?"

She made her decision. If he was going to try to be nice, far be it from her not to let him. Besides, there were times she did ache to lean on someone, for however short a period.

"Lead the way. And Justin?"

"Yes?" He braced himself for another parry.

"Thank you."

His face softened at the unexpected words. "You're welcome," he muttered.

What the hell was he doing to himself? he wondered, helping her into the car. She was right. Mallory could drive her. *She* could drive herself.

Then, refusing to analyze his actions, Justin turned on the ignition.

Chapter Ten

"Are visits to the doctor always like that?" Justin made a right onto the street that led to his aunt's estate. The trip to the pediatrician had been a unique experience for him. The waiting room had been filled to overflowing with mothers either holding coughing, sneezing children, or chasing after children who looked far too healthy to be in a doctor's office in the first place.

He looked in his rearview mirror. That was not the case with Ricky. Dozing, the little boy looked pale. The slight rattling coming from his chest told Justin that Ricky's breathing was labored. Poor little guy.

Her seat belt felt constraining. Philadelphia had adjusted it to accommodate her and Ricky because the little boy refused to settle anywhere but in the comfort of her arms. She glanced up and saw Justin's eyes in the rearview mirror. What was she to make of this man who blew hot and cold? Who kissed her, then went off to his desk "to work"?

Who acted like a remote stranger and then raced to drive her son to the doctor? "Like what?"

A car whizzed by them, and Justin focused his attention on the road again. "Noisy."

She wanted desperately to move, to stretch her body or shift just a little in her seat. But she was afraid of waking Ricky. "Yes, pretty much so. You know, you really didn't have to come."

"You said that already."

Was that hurt she heard in his voice? "But I'm glad you did." A grunt met her words. "You know, you're a very nice man, Justin, when you want to be."

"Why do you sound so surprised, and what do you mean, when I want to be?"

In his sleep, Ricky grabbed her sweater and tugged, pressing it against his cheek. She looked down and suddenly realized what he was doing. With mounting alarm, Philadelphia looked around on both sides of the seat. "Oh no."

"What?" Justin turned his head, hearing the note of abject distress in her voice. At the blast of a horn he had to return his attention to the road in time to avoid swerving into the next lane and into the truck that was coming from the opposite direction.

She felt around along the floor of the car, straining against the seat belt. Nothing. "It's gone."

Heart pounding from the near collision, he didn't risk trying to meet her eyes again in the mirror. "What's gone?"

"Mr. Tiger."

"Who?"

"Mr. Tiger," Philadelphia whispered, afraid of waking Ricky. Once he discovered the loss, there would be no consoling him. Her mind raced as she tried to remember where she had put the new one she had bought. Maybe he'd accept it this time. "His stuffed animal."

Was that what this was all about? Justin wondered. "Give him another stuffed animal."

Philadelphia gritted her teeth. That's probably how he replaced people in his life. What was she doing, she thought irritably, getting involved with a man with no heart? Didn't he understand that things like that couldn't be replaced? The love that went into that bedraggled toy couldn't be found just anywhere.

"It's not that simple. Mr. Tiger is his favorite. He takes it everywhere. It's like Linus and his blanket." Damn, why hadn't she been paying more attention? But she had been so worried about Ricky, she hadn't noticed anything else.

Justin pulled onto the estate's path. As he pressed a button on the panel of his car, the tall iron gates parted. "Did he have it with him when he went to the doctor?"

"Of course, he had it. He dropped it in the driveway and you picked it up, remember? You had that peculiar look on your face."

"It smelled," he answered defensively. He stopped the car before the front door and got out. "Okay, did he have it at the doctor's?"

She undid the seat belt, thinking. "Yes, I think so." Justin opened her door. He seemed to all but fill the available space next to her as he leaned in and gently took Ricky. Philadelphia sighed. She liked the way that looked, Justin holding her son.

Don't get carried away yet, she warned herself. But it was too late for that. She was already gone.

Justin tried not to stare as she got out. Her skirt had hiked up on one side, exposing an ample view of a long slender leg. For such a petite woman, she seemed to be all leg.

Mental images began to tease him. This wasn't the time, he reminded himself.

But it would never be the time. "Call the doctor's office and see if it's still there. I'm sure no one would have willingly taken that thing."

Frowning, Philadelphia put out her arms to take Ricky, but Justin ignored her gesture and simply began walking toward the house. "I'll take him to his room," Justin told her.

She walked quickly beside him. "Thank you."

Justin turned his head, looking straight in front of him. He needed to get away from her smile, from the warm look in her eyes. She was doing things to him again, and he didn't want that. He knew what she was thinking, and she was wrong. He was just being a good human being, nothing more. There was nothing between them. There was no basis for a relationship, nothing. The need to keep repeating this to himself rather than to her annoyed him. He had no idea why he had to keep reminding himself of something he inherently believed. With luck, there might be a friendship in this—if he didn't strangle her first.

Justin turned in his bed and looked at the luminous dials on his clock. Three a.m. He was close to giving up on getting any sleep that night. Every time his own thoughts stopped nagging him, the cries would start again. Whimpers that broke into wails and then subsided into heart-wrenching sobs. Oddly enough, the irritation that should have erupted at this grating disturbance didn't. Justin found himself more concerned about Ricky than the fact that he wasn't getting any sleep.

He might have known she'd have a kid who stayed up nights crying, he thought, searching fruitlessly for a trace of vexation. There wasn't any, not with Ricky, at any rate.

He sat up in bed and ran his hand through his hair, catching a glimpse of himself in the mirror. His hair wasn't perfect the way *she* had sarcastically told Rosalind that it was. Besides, he grumbled, what was wrong with looking well-groomed? She usually looked as if she had just sprung out of bed. A bed still warm from the imprint of her body....

Lack of sleep was making his thoughts ramble.

Kicking the covers aside, Justin got out of bed and pulled his robe over his bare chest, tying it loosely about his waist. As an afterthought, he secured his sinking pajama bottoms and went out into the hall, forgetting his slippers. It wasn't like him.

He rapped on Philadelphia's door twice before she opened it. She probably couldn't hear above the noise, he thought. When she opened it, she looked just the way he thought she would, her hair every which way, her robe hanging open, something he had once heard referred to as a shortie night-gown just skimming the tops of her thighs. He felt his body tighten and gave up the last prayer of ever getting any sleep tonight. "What's the matter with Ricky?"

Until five seconds ago, Philadelphia had felt incredibly punchy. She had walked the floor with Ricky all night, hoping to calm him down. The medicine the doctor had prescribed was supposed to put him to sleep, but the child wasn't taking it. Since Mr. Tiger had been lost, he was inconsolable.

The back of Philadelphia's mind registered the fact that Justin had a much more muscular chest than she would have thought. The ties of his robe were coming undone. He looked considerably more rugged than he had the first time she had met him....

She shifted Ricky's head slightly on her shoulder, feeling as if her arms were going to break. "He won't take his medicine. He keeps crying for Mr. Tiger." Stroking his head for a moment, she linked her hands again beneath the little body. Who would have ever thought that twenty-two pounds would have felt so heavy?

"You should have bought a spare."

"I *do* have a spare." It was hard not to sound waspish. Her nerves were worn, and she was worried.

Justin felt as though he had been kicked in the stomach. The vulnerable look in her eyes came as a surprise. He wouldn't have thought anything could rattle her. She looked worried, lost. Helpless. He realized that he didn't want her to feel that way. "So what's the problem?"

She shrugged helplessly. "He won't accept it. He knows the difference."

"Let me see it."

She had no idea what good that would do, but she went and picked up the toy from the bed where Ricky had tossed it. "Here." She shoved it at Justin.

Justin turned the tiger around carefully. "Looks too clean. No wonder he won't believe it's his." Holding the tiger by his tail, Justin turned around and walked away, leaving her utterly bewildered. As she watched, Justin headed for the stairs.

Curious, she went after him, cradling Ricky against her. "Where are you going?"

He didn't bother turning around. "To perform surgery."

He wasn't making any sense. Even for him. "What?" She had to hurry to keep up with him.

Light flooded the kitchen when he turned on the switch. Philadelphia blinked twice as her eyes adjusted to the brightness. Ricky wailed louder. "Shhhh." She rocked from side to side, attempting to soothe him.

In the glare of the overhead light, Justin realized that Philadelphia's long robe was see-through. She had her back to him, and there was something entirely too erotic about the silhouette of her legs as they joined with her torso. He reminded himself that he was on a mission of mercy. Missions of mercy did not involve X-rated thoughts. Muttering under his breath, he pulled a pair of scissors out of the drawer.

"Make sure he doesn't see," he cautioned in a low voice. He wanted to add a request that she stand out in the hall, but didn't.

Philadelphia kept her back to Justin, although she glanced over her shoulder to see what he was doing. Ricky's head was buried against her chest, and he was sobbing and hiccuping. Philadelphia's eyes grew wide as she watched Justin plunge the scissors into the tiger's body. Had he gone crazy?

"Justin—"

"I know what I'm doing," he told her calmly.

That made one of them, she thought, watching uncertainly. As she stared, Justin began to yank stuffing out of the slight opening he had made in the tiger. The toy began to lose its pudgy appearance until, finally, the animal was a shell of its former self. Justin examined it, nodded his satisfaction, then opened up the cabinet beneath the sink. Tilting the garbage pail toward him, he gingerly moved things around with his free hand.

Why in heaven's name was he rummaging through the garbage? Philadelphia seated herself at the table, too tired to stand any longer. She rocked in a constant rhythm in the hopes that Ricky would be lulled to sleep. "Now what?"

He thought he had seen Angie toss the soiled aluminum foil right on the top. Apparently not. "Angie made yams tonight."

Philadelphia decided it was possible that screaming children made him lose his senses. "So?"

"She always overbakes yams. There's always this glob of burnt sugar that oozes out of them."

"Sounds delicious." Philadelphia winced. Ricky was beginning to fuss again, and her patience was hanging by a thread. "I still don't see—"

"Ah!" It appeared he found what he was looking for. Philadelphia leaned closer to get a better view of what this madman was up to. Taking a black, crisp bubble into his fingers, he liberally applied it to the newly slenderized Mr. Tiger's face. The crust broke and smudged the wide grin. Justin rubbed the rest along the striped body. Bright orange turned a faded, muddy brown. It was beginning to look exactly like Ricky's missing tiger.

Philadelphia grinned to herself. You just never knew, did you?

"Hush, Ricky, it's going to be just fine," she murmured as Ricky sent up another wail. She put out her hand for the destroyed tiger, but Justin was once again looking for something. This time he was pulling out drawers. "What are you doing now?"

"Looking for this." He held up a plastic bag. Mr. Tiger was deposited inside. Philadelphia watched him knot it at one end.

"Um, Justin, I think he's dead already. There's no need to smother him."

He wasn't listening. "It needs something more. I'll be right back."

As Justin disappeared into the garage, Philadelphia rolled her eyes. Was he planning on taking the tiger out for a ride? What was the matter with him?

A couple of moments later, she heard the sound of a car being started up. He *was* taking the tiger for a ride. "I think the man has lost his mind, Ricky." Ricky sobbed. "Oh, baby, why won't you take your medicine? You'll feel all better if you do.''

Ricky responded by burying his face deeper into her now-soggy shoulder. Too tired to get up, Philadelphia stayed where she was, rocking him gently against her body.

Five minutes later, Justin returned, holding Mr. Tiger, a squashed Mr. Tiger, aloft.

"You found him?" she asked, delighted.

"No, I ran him over."

"Would you repeat that, please?"

He almost laughed at the bewildered look on her face. *So, how does it feel to have the shoe on the other foot and not understand a thing that's being said?*

"As I recall," Justin said, "Ricky's Mr. Tiger had a very flattened appearance. So I ran the car over him a few times." Justin discarded the plastic bag and tossed it on the table. "Now, for the final touch." Sticking the tiger under one arm, he opened the pantry and hunted until he uncovered the vinegar.

She watched him uncork the bottle. "I'm not even going to ask."

"That's a first." Justin sprinkled a little vinegar on the tiger.

She couldn't stand it any longer. "All right—what are you doing?"

"Mr. Tiger also had a certain aroma as you pointed out. Children are very quick to pick up on things like that."

He replaced the bottle on the shelf and noticed that she was smiling for the first time tonight. The corners of her eyes crinkled, and he felt himself being drawn to her smile.

"And what makes you such an expert on children?" she asked, amused.

"They tell me I was one myself once."

She remembered what Rosalind had told her. "Did you have a Mr. Tiger?"

"Not exactly. I had a rabbit."

"That's right," she said, remembering. He had mentioned having a stuffed animal. "What did you call him?"

"Rabbit."

"Imaginative."

"Not like Mr. Tiger, right?"

She laughed, suddenly not feeling tired anymore. "Point taken."

"He looked a lot like this. Kind of smelled like this, too." His voice dropped just a little, but she noticed. "My mother gave him to me."

She reached out and touched his arm. "Oh, Justin."

Embarrassed by what he saw in her eyes, he turned his attention to Ricky. Justin held the tiger near the boy's face. "I think I found a friend of yours, Rick."

Listlessly, the boy raised his head. Then, though his eyes were red with fever, Ricky seemed to come to life. "Mr. Tiger!" His hands darted out to snare his long lost friend.

Justin looked on with satisfaction. It pleased him to be needed, to do something so small and yet so important to one little soul. Helping the masses couldn't hold a candle to this. A part of him that had been shut off opened up. The gratification was not to be described.

Philadelphia felt her heart burst. Now maybe she could get medicine into Ricky. "The operation was a success, Doctor," Philadelphia whispered, getting up slowly. Ricky nestled happily against her, rubbing the tiger against his cheek. Some of the burnt sugar came off on his face. Philadelphia was too relieved to care.

Impulsively, she raised herself up on her bare toes and kissed Justin's cheek. "Thank you."

Justin looked from Ricky to Philadelphia. For just one moment, they were a unit. A family. He knew that it wouldn't continue this way, but there was no reason why, just for now, he couldn't savor the sensation.

Still, her gratitude made him feel awkward. He shrugged, as if what he had done was quite ordinary, done for selfish reasons. "I figured I wouldn't get a good night's sleep until he was reunited with his toy."

"Make all the excuses you want, Justin Starbuck, you can't fool me." She turned and walked out of the kitchen. The smile she had given him lingered in the air.

"I'm not trying to fool you," he called after her.

It was himself, he realized, that he was trying to delude.

He was going to keep to his room until Rosalind was ready to return to the hospital. He was going to occupy himself with things that pertained to the Foundation and to Rosalind. That was the plan he came up with the next morning.

The plan lasted less than an hour.

Time and again, he left the protective shelter of his PC and his fax machine and sought Philadelphia out under some pretext. Three times he asked about Ricky's condition. Twice he fetched her for Rosalind. And if he wasn't walking into a room with her in it, he was walking into a room where she had just been, having left a tantalizing trace of her perfume to tempt him, make him think, make him want.

He tried harder. He failed more completely. She occupied every corner of his mind, every crevice of his heart. He couldn't rid himself of her image. By evening, he had given up the battle, if not the ultimate war.

Drawn by some instinct that told him he would find her there, he walked into the kitchen and discovered Philadelphia up to her elbows in flour. "What are you doing?"

She pushed her hair out of her eyes with the back of her wrist. A white mark streaked her forehead. "Rosalind wanted something sweet."

He looked around. "Where's Angie?"

Her fingers sticky with dough, Philadelphia reached for an egg. Cracking it against the side of the table, she pushed the shell in with her thumb. Egg white shot out, joined by orangey yolk. "It's her day off."

"Good thing she can't see this," he commented, dropping down on a chair next to the scene of the crime. "Don't you have a day off?"

"There's nothing I want to do that isn't here." She looked up at him significantly.

"Like playing with flour?"

"Like trying to make Rosalind a dessert that won't give her or the doctor heart failure. He wants no fats or salt to come within ten feet of her."

That sounded right, but Justin couldn't recall when the doctor had said it. "When did he say that?"

"When I called him to see about her menu."

He might have known. Thorough. He had to admit that he did admire someone being thorough. Especially when that someone came with long, silky blond hair and eyes so green they made him think of a meadow in the springtime.

Justin rested his chin on the back of the chair he was straddling. "So what are you making?"

"It's my own recipe for cookies."

"Need help?"

"You could put some more flour in the bowl for me. My hands are too sticky."

He glanced at them. "So they are."

Justin reached for the sack. Turning it over, he shook the contents out a bit too briskly. A billowing white cloud engulfed them until they both began coughing. The sack toppled over, emptying. The air was thick with flour. She had no choice but to back up. So did Justin. They bumped into each other, and without thinking, Philadelphia grabbed him in order to steady herself. White dough smeared on Justin's light blue pullover. She knew she should apologize, but all she could do was laugh. Helplessly. When she could finally speak, she said, "I guess this kind of ends our dreams of being a bake-off team."

His hands had slipped down to her waist. "You've got flour all over your face."

He picked up a towel from the table and began to wipe away the smudges. The strokes were short, gentle. The towel dropped from his fingers. He framed her face in his hands, utterly incapable of fighting the attraction that was ravaging him. He wanted to fight it, wanted to stave it off, knowing that only disappointment lay ahead. It didn't matter. Not at this moment, not when she looked so very appealing. Not when he wanted to get lost in her kisses.

Philadelphia wasn't fighting anything. She had already accepted the fact that she was falling in love and let herself enjoy the sensation. It felt a lot like an explosion of flowers suddenly in bloom. She hadn't been looking for love or commitment, but now that it was here, she had no intention of running from it. She welcomed it, welcomed the warmth it brought. Welcomed Justin into her heart.

She moved her head, tilting it up to his. "Are you going to kiss me or examine the quality of the flour?"

"Do I have a choice?"

"No."

"Why should this be any different?" He was beginning to doubt that he had had a choice since the moment he had met her.

His mouth fit over hers so well, as if that was what it had been created for. As if he hadn't lived until the moment she had come like gangbusters into his life.

His hunger exploded all the more quickly because he knew what was waiting for him, knew that the taste of her lips, the scent of her breath drove him way beyond the brink of common sense to a place where only madness dwelled. When he felt her tremble against him, the power that surged through him sent his mind reeling. Questions formed, answers came, all swirling away in a vapor. Nothing mattered except this isolated moment in time.

Yes, she thought. Yes! Any doubts she had about him disappeared. He might protest verbally, but the truth was here, in the way he held her, in the way their ragged breaths mingled. "Soul mates," Rosalind had called them. Rosalind was right.

But even as her passion ignited, Philadelphia could feel Justin drawing away. "Justin, what's the matter?"

He took a step back, badly shaken. "This is wrong."

"What do you mean, 'wrong'?" A sharp image of Mark's mother flashed through her mind. Mark's mother saying that his being with her was wrong, that she was wrong for him. Was Justin like that? Tied to some social scale, some preconceived standard that she had no part in?

Justin put distance between them, distance to keep from touching her again, from taking her here and now. "Philadelphia, this isn't going to work between us."

She tried to keep the pain from her voice. "Not if you run from it, no."

He hated it when she looked like that. He didn't want to hurt her. But she would hurt him. They would hurt each other eventually. "You don't understand."

Calmly, she walked to the sink and let the water run over her hands. She scrubbed the dough from her fingers. Her voice was low. "I understand that I wasn't looking for love, but now that it's found me, I intend to stay found."

He pulled her around by her shoulder. "Love?"

Philadelphia never wavered as she looked up into his eyes. "Love."

In helpless anger, he let go of her. "You don't know what you're talking about."

She sighed in exasperation. Why couldn't he just let this happen? She cared. She *knew* he did. "I know exactly what I'm talking about. You're the one who's confused, not me."

"Are you always so sure of yourself?"

"I am in this instance."

He looked at her, for a moment believing her, believing that lasting relationships were possible.

But then he knew he was just wishing that it were true, because of her. Hadn't his father approached his marriages in the same fashion? "This one is going to be forever." Justin had heard that so many times. Forever had a very short life expectancy.

"I've got to get back to work." His voice rang hollow in his ears.

Philadelphia figured she had a choice. She could get angry or she could get practical. Sometimes it paid to think like the opposition. All was fair in love and war, and this, it seemed, was both.

She took off the apron she was wearing and placed it on the back of the chair. The cookies were going to have to wait. This was more important. Much more important. "It's not going anywhere."

Her words stopped him as he crossed to the doorway. "What isn't?"

"Your work."

Justin turned around. "But I have to—"

Philadelphia put on her largest smile. "Rosalind says you're a workaholic."

"I am not."

She continued as if he hadn't said anything. Easily, she linked her arm through his. When it sagged, she pushed it back up so that her arm remained in the crook of his. "But it's not your fault. You're a Capricorn. They're supposed to be ambitious workaholics."

For a moment, he permitted himself to be led astray. "You go in for this mumbo jumbo of hers?"

"I didn't, but it seems to me that what she's been saying about you has been pretty much on the mark with the material she's given me to read."

He'd never met a woman with so much mischief in her eyes. "And what has she been saying about me?"

"Among other things, that you shy away from a one-on-one relationship."

Justin stiffened. "That's not because of my sign. That's because of the things I've seen happen in my life."

The shrug of her shoulders dismissed his justification. "Just excuses."

"I don't need excuses."

"No, you don't." Philadelphia smiled up into his face and for a moment, Justin didn't breathe. "You don't need anything at all."

She put her hand into his and tugged. "C'mon, Justin. It's a nice night and you need the air." She waved her hand around the kitchen, as if to dispel the lingering cloud of flour.

He knew when he was outmatched. He'd give in to her on this one small point. Maybe it would appease her.

And maybe, he thought as he followed her out, it would just make her want more.

As it did him.

Chapter Eleven

She created a peacefulness within him even as she excited him. How could whirling chaos evoke tranquility? He didn't understand. He only knew that she did. She was full of contradictions, yet was somehow the most stable person Justin had ever met besides Rosalind.

"Justin, are you okay?" Woody's voice echoed in the receiver after one particular lapse of silence went too long.

Justin looked at the telephone and mentally upbraided himself. He had been looking out his window, watching Philadelphia talk to Mallory. He had no idea what she was saying, but she was gesturing in the air with every word. No doubt about it, the woman was animated.

He'd never felt the need to alter his life to accommodate another. He had thought he had it all mapped out, devoting himself to the Foundation. The Foundation was doing a lot of good in the country, and there was talk of branching out into Mexico and the Philippines. The Foundation made a difference. Yet now he found himself yearning to make a difference with one person. Just one person.

He was an idiot.

"Justin? Are you there?"

A complete, consummate idiot. He glanced down at the notes on his pad. "Sorry, Woody, just thinking."

"When are you coming back? These last four days have felt like four years. How the hell do you keep up the pace?"

"Vitamins." Now he was being flippant. Like her. He didn't know if he was making a difference to her, but she certainly was to him.

"Well, send me some. I'm going to need about a case to tide me over until you get back. Sam Falwell needs an answer by—"

"There's nothing going on that you can't handle, Woody," Justin said calmly. Four days ago he wouldn't have even considered saying that. Now he didn't feel quite so indispensable. "My aunt's surgery has been postponed for a couple of days. Seems she caught a cold." Again, he waited for the feeling of impatience to get back to his work. It didn't come. He was almost grateful to Ricky for passing on his germs.

Almost? He *was* grateful. It gave him an excuse to remain here. He had promised Rosalind he would stay until after the operation. And he meant to keep his word. For more reasons than one now.

"I'll be back . . ."

He leaned forward to watch as Philadelphia disappeared from view. Why was he stretching just to look at her? What was he hoping to see at a distance that he didn't see close up? Was he searching for a flaw that would make him back away?

No, the truth was, he just wanted to look at her.

"You'll be back when?" Woody prompted.

Justin sat back in his chair. "What?"

There was barely veiled exasperation in Woody's voice. "You started to say when you'd be back, but you didn't finish your sentence.... Justin, are you all right over there?"

Justin realized the man's concern was genuine and wondered why he had never noticed things like that before. Maybe things could have been different if only—

No, things wouldn't have been different. Things were constant. He had seen patterns repeated time and again. "I'm not sure. But I'll be right back after Rosalind's surgery. Should be Monday."

"That means you'll have been gone a whole week," Woody lamented.

Justin laughed at the comical tone. "That's not a lifetime, Woody."

And yet, he thought when he hung up, maybe it was. Maybe a week was a lifetime. He felt as if he had been through a lifetime already. Before Monday, he had been complacent, orderly. Content just the way he was. Now, he didn't know what he was.

Except, possibly, in love.

Was this what it was? He didn't know. He had never been there before. He had never allowed himself to go that route. The relationships he had had with women were superficially satisfying, and when they ended, as they always did, he gave no thought to them. No thoughts, no regrets. Mutually satisfying ventures that terminated when they ceased to be jointly gratifying.

He ran his hand through his hair. God, he sounded as if he was describing business mergers.

Maybe, he thought, that's all they had been. Until now.

She was all wrong for him. She was bossy, headstrong and charged into things without weighing the pros and cons. Yet

Rosalind insisted that she was the one fated to be his. The stars said so. Ha!

He heard a sneeze from down the hall and decided to see how Rosalind was feeling.

"Miserable, that's how," she answered his query a minute later, blowing into a lacy handkerchief. "But at least I have a reprieve from the doctor's revelry. Do you know what I need?"

Justin tried to make himself comfortable on the chaise lounge and found that he couldn't. It was stacked with more of her books. "I haven't the faintest idea." There was nothing predictable about his aunt's notions.

She waved her hand into the air, as if to conjure something up. "Nightgowns."

That sounded simple enough to him. "Have someone buy them for you."

"I am."

"Good."

"You."

He stared at her. There were three other women in the house far more qualified than he to pick something out.

"Me? I don't know the first thing about—"

Rosalind reached for another handkerchief. "Then it's about time that you learned. Take Philadelphia with you and bring me back four, no five different sets. Violets and lavenders. To match my eyes."

She obviously wasn't going to be talked out of this. "This isn't very subtle of you, Aunt Roz."

"I don't want subtle, I want nightgowns. With feathers along the bottom and lacy stitching across the bodice." She raised her eyes to his face. "Please?"

Resting his hands on his knees, he rose. "I never could refuse you."

The smile had her chins dimpling into one another. "I was counting on that. Now go, hurry." She shooed him away with a wave of her wrists.

As Cupid, she wasn't very original, but then, she didn't have to be, Justin thought. She was Rosalind Starbuck, used to getting her own way. If she could, she'd probably order one romance, à la carte for him and Philadelphia.

But it didn't work that way. She above all people should know that. She had seen what he had seen. And even she had never remarried.

He found Philadelphia in the den, a box of old letters next to her on the cluttered desk. She was sobbing her heart out. Without thinking, he crossed to her quickly, pushing back her chair and gathering her in his arms. "What's the matter?"

She looked up, unashamed of the fact that there were tear stains on her cheeks and that her nose was just the slightest bit red. She looked a mess. The most adorable mess he had ever seen.

Justin held her to him and felt the sobs. She was getting his shirt wet, but it didn't seem to matter to him. He stroked her hair, waiting until she got hold of herself. "Is it Ricky?"

She looked disoriented as she drew her head back. "What?"

"Is something wrong with Ricky?"

"Oh no, no." She sniffled, and Justin dug into his pocket and handed her his handkerchief. "Ricky's just fine now. Good as new."

"Then why are you—"

She didn't let him finish. But he had come to expect that. "I was reading a letter from your aunt to your uncle. It was so beautiful. She really loved him."

Was that all? He couldn't understand how that could be the cause of her tears. If he lived forever, he wasn't going to understand this woman. But, he told himself as he moved to the other side of the desk, he wasn't going to have to worry about that. This time next week, they'd be in different worlds again. "Yes, I guess she did. I hadn't really thought about it."

Philadelphia placed the faded letter back onto the stack neatly and sighed. Some of Rosalind's distinctive perfume still clung to the paper. "Renews your faith."

He looked at the scores of boxes in the small paneled room. Rosalind certainly did keep a lot of memorabilia, he thought. "In what?"

Philadelphia tried to remind herself that this was the man who had run a car over a toy tiger for her while dressed in his pajama bottoms. "In everything."

"Not mine."

"Why?" She turned to really look at him. "Don't you have any faith?"

He was thumbing through an old photo album and paused to look at a photo of Rosalind on the set of one of her first movies. Yes, she had been a stunning woman, he thought with a touch of pride. He glanced up, aware that Philadelphia had asked a question. "In what?"

"Life, people, things."

He closed the album with a snap of his wrist and put it down. "You're spouting nonsense again."

"Again?"

He grinned. Anger became her, although, if pressed, he'd have to say he was partial to her smile. "Do you prefer the word *still?*"

"I would prefer the word *murder,* but your aunt might have objections." Philadelphia shoved his handkerchief back at him.

Justin placed it back into his pocket. "Speaking of whom..."

"Yes?"

"Aunt Roz wants us to get her five nightgown sets."

"Peignoir sets?"

"I guess so."

She noticed that he looked vaguely uncomfortable, but shrugged it off. Philadelphia pushed her chair toward the desk, then slung her purse over her shoulder. "How's her cold this afternoon?" Philadelphia felt guilty. If Rosalind hadn't caught Ricky's cold, she would have been going into the hospital today.

"Better. She seems actually happy about being sick." He watched the easy way Philadelphia seemed to move, like a breeze. Maybe more like a gale.

Two steps took her to the door. She paused, waiting for him to join her. "That's because she's afraid of the surgery."

"Afraid? Aunt Roz?"

"Sure. She's human. We'll be gone a couple of hours, Angie," she called out to the woman as they passed in the foyer. "Could you and Margarita look in on Ricky? He's napping right now. He should stay down for another hour or so."

Angie merely nodded and waved them on.

Justin laughed softly, marveling at the ease she seemed to zip in and out of conversations. He shuddered to think what her mind must look like. "I guess I always thought of Aunt Roz as larger than life."

Philadelphia caught the inflection in his voice and wondered if he was aware of it. Probably not. If he was, he wouldn't have allowed it to slip out. "You love her a lot, don't you?"

He was going to say something noncommittal and discovered that he couldn't. For some unapparent reason, he found himself saying a lot to Philadelphia that he never admitted to anyone else.

"Yes, I do. Can we get on with this?" He gestured to the front door.

"I fully intend to."

She wasn't talking about shopping. He knew that. And for a moment, he thought of begging off and saying something about work, but she gave him that knowing look before he could open his mouth.

He took her arm and marshalled her out the door.

With Ricky being taken care of, Philadelphia was quite content to spend the afternoon shopping. Looking at pretty things was one of the joys in life that had been denied her lately. Money had never been plentiful in her life, but after Ricky had been born, Philadelphia had had to husband every cent to pay all the bills. Coming to work for Rosalind had changed all of that. The woman had made very generous provisions for Philadelphia.

To her amused delight, Philadelphia found that Justin was embarrassed by the nature of their shopping spree. She took him from lingerie department to lingerie department in three exclusive stores at the mall, looking for just the right things for Rosalind. He grew increasingly uncomfortable looking at little bits of translucent apparel.

"What do you think of this?" She held up a violet nightgown that was more like a violet cloud than an article of clothing. It was frivolous enough to suit Rosalind, she thought. In fascination, she watched Justin's face color to a pale shade of pink.

"I think she'll catch another cold," he muttered, wishing he were somewhere else.

Philadelphia put it down, tickled. "Apparently, you've never made these kinds of purchases for anyone special in your life."

"There's never been anyone special in my life until—" He stopped himself abruptly.

"Until?" she prodded.

When she lifted her eyebrows like that, they disappeared under her bangs. She looked younger than the twenty-five years he knew she was. "Until Aunt Roz asked me to buy these things."

Philadelphia grinned impishly, still fingering the nightgown. "The end of your sentence doesn't agree with the beginning."

He was finding her increasingly hard to resist. "Suddenly you're a grammarian?"

She laughed out loud, and he finally smiled. There was a saleswoman hovering several feet away from them. He was beginning to feel hemmed in. "Want to get out of here and get something to eat?" he proposed.

"I'd love to, but first, business." And with that, Philadelphia gathered up the last two sets they had looked at and presented them to the saleswoman, who brightened immeasurably.

"Cash or charge?"

"Charge." She handed Rosalind's gold charge plate to the saleswoman. "I've always wanted to say that," she told Justin.

"Don't you have a card?"

"Just for emergencies. So far, luckily, none have come up." She turned back to the saleswoman, missing the thoughtful way Justin was regarding her.

* * *

Why don't you look tired?" Justin asked.

Philadelphia looked up from her drink, surprised by his question. "Because I'm not."

Justin leaned back in the booth. The restaurant was fairly empty. There was little sound around them save the soft piped-in music. It gave him a chance to study her and not look too obvious about it.

"But you were up at dawn, I heard you," he explained in answer to her quizzical expression. "And we've just spent—" he glanced at his watch "—three hours shopping. In between, you were working on Aunt Roz's book. Not to mention taking care of a rather overactive two-year-old. Why aren't you exhausted?"

She shrugged carelessly. "I have natural staying power."

He looked down into the depths of his own glass. The ice was melting into the Scotch, making it watery. It didn't have nearly the kick that one of her kisses did. "Something tells me that I should be careful."

"Don't," she urged, placing her hand on his wrist. She felt it tense, then relax beneath her fingers. "Don't be careful. Take a risk, just once." She hesitated only an instant before she continued. "I like the way you look at me, Justin."

There were no games with her. He appreciated honesty. So why did it scare the hell out of him at the same time? "Do you always say everything you think?"

"Usually. I've got a mouth that gets me into trouble."

It gets me into trouble, too, Justin thought, remembering the way her lips felt against his.

"But I don't believe in holding things back. It's one of my faults, I suppose, but I can't help it. It also frightens people away sometimes."

She sounded sad when she said it. Her anger fascinated him, her laughter made him feel warm. He didn't like seeing sadness in her eyes. "I can understand that. You frighten the hell out of me."

"Do I?"

"Absolutely."

"Why?"

"Because you have a way of looking at me that makes me forget." He was saying too much, but he couldn't stop. Maybe her affliction was catching.

She cocked her head, her hair spilling over one shoulder. "Forget? Forget what?"

"That I promised myself never to fall into the same trap that my father keeps falling into." He tilted the stocky glass in his hand, looking at the amber liquid. "Sixty-three years old and he's looking for another wife. His seventh. Sixth, if you don't count the fact that he married Julie twice—before and after Evelyn." He laughed, but there was no laughter in his eyes. "When I was a kid, I always wanted to send someone a Mother's Day card, but didn't know to who or how many I should send. Until Aunt Roz."

"She's a very special lady."

"Well..." He tried to dismiss the mood that he had unwittingly created. "At least we're agreed on that."

She sensed him withdrawing again. For a moment, she felt her temper rearing its head. Why did he have to keep doing this? Why couldn't he just stay open with her? She wanted nothing from him except...things he wouldn't give, she thought sadly. "Oh, I think we agree on more than that. We're more alike than you'd like to admit."

He raised an eyebrow at that. "You run headlong into life. I test the water."

The point she was trying to make was forgotten in the face of his tone. "I commit."

He knew what she was saying. That he was afraid of commitment. And he didn't care for the criticism. "You should be committed. To an institution." He had never met anyone who could make him lose his temper the way she did. And then regret it just as fast.

"I am," she answered quietly. Out of the corner of her eye, she saw a waiter approach, then hurry away. Apparently he had caught some of this exchange. "The institution is called marriage."

"That's not what I meant, and I'm . . ." He'd been about to apologize and wasn't sure what had come over him.

"That's all too evident."

His apology evaporated. "Meaning?"

"That you're afraid to commit."

"No, I'm afraid of what happens *after* I commit. I'm not a dreamer, Philadelphia. I won't shut out reality and make my father's mistakes."

"There's nothing wrong in dreaming, Justin. Sometimes dreams come true."

"'Sometimes' isn't good enough."

"Life doesn't come with guarantees. Surely someone as practical as you knows that."

His anger was gone now. This was something they wouldn't resolve. He already knew that, knew that even as they had argued. "How is it that you can twist everything I believe in so that it doesn't sound right?"

At the sound of subdued voices, the waiter approached them with their orders, placed them on the table quickly and left.

"It's a gift." She grinned.

"That wasn't the word I had in mind."

He watched her as she sipped her wine. He watched her long, slender fingers glide along the stem and thought of the way those fingers would feel against his skin, touching, probing. He couldn't dismiss the image. Nor the desire. He had no doubts that when Roz's surgery was finally over, he'd leave, return to his world and never see Philadelphia again. He didn't believe in relationships, he reminded himself.

Mallory brought them back to the estate. No sooner did he stop the limousine that Philadelphia was out, racing into the house to see Ricky.

"Just like a woman," Justin muttered, looking at the packages she had left for him to bring in.

"She certainly is, isn't she?"

The wistful sigh and grin on Mallory's face told Justin they did not have the same thing in mind.

Justin and Mallory brought the packages into Rosalind's bedroom. It was hard finding a place for the boxes amid the flowers and plants that had taken over every free space in the room. Philadelphia was already there and moved things around to create a little opening. She smiled triumphantly at Justin, then proceeded to hand the various boxes to Rosalind for the woman's scrutiny.

But Rosalind was obviously far more interested in the byplay between Justin and Philadelphia than in anything they had brought to her.

A profusion of colors covered Rosalind's king-size bed. She nodded her approval. "You surprise me, Justin. These are really lovely."

He had never been one to take credit where none was due. "I had nothing to do with it. It was all Philadelphia's doing. She dragged me from one store to another."

"I had no idea you were such a stuffed shirt, Justin." She turned toward Philadelphia and frowned. "Why aren't you seeing about getting him a little more humanized?"

"It's not an easy task, but I'm doing my best, Rosalind."

"According to my readings—" the older woman tapped a book on her nightstand "—you should bring out the best in him."

"Well, there your readings are wrong," Justin told her. "Whenever I'm around Miss Whirlwind, I— What are you laughing at?"

Rosalind had her hand to her chest as it heaved. "You. The stars are never wrong, Justin. I think you've met your match."

Suddenly, the laughter faded as the color drained from her face.

The wordplay was forgotten. Justin was at her side instantly. "What's the matter?"

Rosalind pressed her lips together. "Just a twinge. My pills..."

Philadelphia was already shaking one out of the container Rosalind kept close at hand. "Here, put this under your tongue," she instructed.

Rosalind did as she was told. In a moment, she sighed. The tension left her shoulders as she sank back against the pillows. "Better."

Justin shook his head. It had been a scare. One he didn't want to relive. He began to appreciate what Philadelphia must have gone through the morning his aunt had had her attack. "It won't be better until you've had that surgery."

Sensing he wanted some time alone with his aunt, Philadelphia retreated. "I'd better get back to Ricky before he drives Angie crazy."

Rosalind nodded her consent, then looked up at Justin. The man looked so much better when he smiled, she thought. "Don't be in such a hurry to get rid of me."

"I'm not. That's why I want that surgery. I want you around for a long, long time." He stacked the boxes together and put them all on the floor, out of the way.

She peered at him. "Long enough to see grandnieces and nephews?"

Satisfied that things were in some semblance of order, he turned his attention back to Rosalind. "There's a little boy running around the estate now. Isn't that enough for you?"

"No," she said frankly, reaching for his hand. He wrapped his fingers around hers. It was a strong hand. A gentle hand. Philadelphia had told her about the episode with the stuffed tiger and the car. He'd make a good father. But then, she had always known that. "I want more. I want you happy."

Justin gave her hand an affectionate squeeze. "I am happy."

But she knew better. "No. You're existing." Her voice rose, carrying the dramatic surge she was known for. "I want one wonderful, glorious love in your life for you."

Gently, he separated his hand from hers, patting it as he eased it down on the comforter that covered her. "Don't get yourself excited," he cautioned.

"No, I want *you* excited."

He crossed to the door. "I'll see what I can do about it."

Rosalind pointed to the left. It was a gesture worthy of an empress. "Second door down the hall."

Justin laughed, shaking his head. "You're incorrigible."

"They always told me that." She winked and settled back on the pillows, content that things would turn out the way they were supposed to.

Chapter Twelve

Philadelphia opened her eyes, focused in on her digital clock and bolted upright. Seven o'clock!

Why hadn't Ricky called out to her? He was always up by six at the very latest. Something was wrong.

Kicking off her covers, she made one attempt to find her slippers, failed and gave up. She grabbed her robe and hurried to the next room, chewing her lower lip.

Had he had a relapse? It wasn't like him to sleep this late. She wasn't cut out for this mother thing, she thought in exasperation. Too many worries.

Philadelphia pushed the hair out of her eyes as she raced into the hallway. Her robe barely hung on her body, the sash flapping uselessly about her middle. She flew into Ricky's room, only to find his bed empty. "Ricky?"

She looked around the room, but there were few places where he could hide. He wasn't there.

She was about to run down the stairs, hoping that perhaps Angie had him with her when she heard his high-pitched voice laughing.

"More, more, more, Dusdin."

Dusdin? Who the heck was Dusdin? And what was he doing with her child?

Philadelphia swung around and then realized that her son's voice was coming from Justin's room.

"Dusdin," she said aloud. "Of course."

Fears subsided and curiosity arose. She quietly approached Justin's room, not wanting to interrupt. She nudged the partially-opened door just enough to be able to see into the room. Justin and Ricky were on the floor, deep in conversation. Justin was sitting cross-legged with the boy propped up against his body. They were discussing the oversized storybook that Justin held opened in front of him. Mr. Tiger lay at their feet, keeping guard.

Justin pretended to be stern as he looked down into the round, sunny face. It wasn't easy. Ricky had all of Philadelphia's features in miniature, right down to the extraordinarily long, sooty lashes that framed round, expressive green eyes. "We've already read three stories, Rick."

"More."

Justin sighed. "I see logic doesn't mean anything to you, either. Just like your mother, huh? Good at giving orders."

Philadelphia stifled a laugh. She noted that Ricky's hair was neatly combed and he was dressed in red corduroy rompers and a bright, electric-blue shirt.

She felt her heart warming. Her instincts had been right, after all. Hers *and* Rosalind's, she added as an afterthought.

Ricky tugged at the book, pushing it higher in front of Justin's face. "More."

Justin laughed softly, ruffling the hair he had taken such pains to get right. Combing a moving target was far more difficult than he had thought. "And a one-track mind. Also like your mother."

"Mo—"

"Yes, I get the picture. More. Okay, sport." He shifted Ricky so that his weight was more evenly distributed on his leg, which was beginning to fall asleep. "But just one more and then it's time to wake up your mom. She's going to turn into a lazy slugabed." That would be the day, he thought with a grin.

Philadelphia wanted to go on watching the two of them together, but felt it was time to rescue Justin. She walked into the room.

"Mom's already awake."

Justin's head jerked up as she crossed toward them. From his vantage point, he received a very arousing, very tempting view of her shortie nightgown and what was concealed, or rather, not concealed beneath it. The smooth skin made him suddenly aware of an uncomfortable, demanding itch. "And so am I," he muttered under his breath.

Justin cleared his throat. "He was calling for you. I was already awake so I decided to see what he needed."

Storybook forgotten, Ricky lifted his arms to be picked up. "Momma."

Philadelphia obliged, tucking him against her. Justin noticed how effortlessly she held the wiggly weight.

"Funny, I usually wake up when he calls." She added silently that she didn't usually oversleep, either.

Justin closed the storybook. "Maybe if you went to bed like normal people, you'd get enough sleep to get up at the crack of dawn."

"Why, Justin—" she looked down at him, grinning "—I didn't know you cared."

Why didn't she leave and get dressed already? he wondered, agitated. There was only so much temptation a man could successfully resist. "I just like peace and quiet, and crying children are not integral to peace and quiet."

Philadelphia shifted Ricky's weight. She wasn't about to let Justin talk his way out of this one. "So you got him up, dressed him and read to him." She looked closer at the sunny, smiling face. There was still a trace of jam at the corners of the boy's mouth. "And fed him, I see."

Justin rose to his feet, holding Mr. Tiger. He tucked the toy under Ricky's arm. Why was she making such a big production out of this? He only did the natural thing.

Yes, but not just to satisfy Ricky, a small voice said.

"He was hungry." Unconsciously, Justin rubbed his thigh, trying to get the feeling back. The rest of him, unfortunately, was feeling much too much.

Well, he decided, if she wouldn't leave, he would. The room had gotten ten degrees hotter since she walked in, her legs up to the neck, her nightgown nonexistent, looking like every man's fantasy. He started to pass her, but Ricky didn't let him get away. The boy grabbed onto the cuff of Justin's sweater.

"More, Dusdin, more."

"Dusdin will read to you later, Ricky, after he gets over his embarrassment at being found out."

"Being found out as what?"

"As an incredibly nice human being."

"Because I fed him? You seem to forget, Ms. Jones, I feed a lot of people in my line of work."

Holding Ricky with one arm propped under his behind, Philadelphia smoothed out a wrinkle in Justin's turtleneck. "I'm not forgetting." She raised her eyes to his and smiled deeply. So deeply that he thought he was going to fall in and get lost. "And you seem just to be remembering."

He took her hand. He meant to push it aside. He had never liked hands fussing over him; his governesses had always fussed, straightened, tugged. But he caught himself holding her hand too long in his. Because it felt so right. "What's that supposed to mean?"

She noticed the hesitation and was glad. She turned her palm up and linked her fingers through his. "That I think you're finally dropping your barriers and getting in touch with your feelings and with people. Rosalind said that that was part of your sign, too, but only if someone pushed you toward it."

One eyebrow arched. She felt like lightly touching it with her lips.

"And that someone was you?" he asked.

"Why, thank you."

Justin frowned. "That was a sarcastic question, not a compliment."

She laughed. Ricky wiggled, wanting to get down, and she let him go.

Justin watched her bend over, unconsciously exposing considerable cleavage. He felt another surge of desire. He told himself that it was just a normal physical reaction, that he wasn't, after all, made out of stone. But it wasn't just that. There was more, much more. He wanted to hold her, to gently caress her face. To...

Time to leave.

"I take what I can get," Philadelphia said.

It took a moment to push his heart out of his throat after he shifted his gaze. "And twist it."

Taking the lead, she threaded her hands around his waist. Some horses, she decided, you had to lead to water. "If necessary." She smiled. "There's absolutely nothing wrong with liking children, Justin."

Every time he was near her like this, his body took on a life of its own, making demands that were getting harder and harder to ignore. For a moment, he let himself hold her, enjoying the softness, the feel and the smell of her. "It's not a habit I want to cultivate. Just as liking you is something I don't want to encourage."

"This is getting to sound interesting." She turned her face up to his. "Tell me more."

The robe was hardly on her shoulders. He wanted to strip it from her entirely. Perhaps if Ricky hadn't been in the room, he might have. He didn't know, and he didn't want to debate the possibility. The fact was that the boy *was* there, rustling pages in his storybook. Justin discovered that he couldn't think clearly anymore. Philadelphia occupied every corner of his mind.

His hands were underneath her robe and he pulled her closer to him. Her warm, soft body tantalized him, reminded him that he hadn't kissed her in over a day and that nothing mattered more than that. As if they had a mind of their own, he felt his hands reaching up higher, until the tips of his fingers caressed the sides of her breasts. Her sharp intake of breath stimulated him. As if he needed it.

"I believe," he corrected her, "that the expression is 'show me.'"

"That, too," she murmured against his mouth, and let herself do what came naturally. He kissed her long and hard, with an urgency that totally demolished her ability to breathe, to think, to stand on her own power. She clung to his shoulders. Her knees had ceased to exist.

This wasn't enough, he thought. It would never be enough. He needed her and wanted her, and he knew what happened after that. He'd be lost, waiting for the inevitable. Beads of perspiration formed on his brow as he tried to shake himself free of the overwhelming power she seemed to have over him.

Literally shaking, he pulled away. For one moment, he'd virtually forgotten about the child at his feet, about promises made to himself, about never being involved and never hurting.

But Philadelphia couldn't let go of his shoulders. Not immediately. Not if she didn't want to slide down to the floor. Slowly, she opened her hands, withdrawing her fingertips, testing the strength in her legs. They held. But just barely.

"I have to go," he told her, his voice deep, his breathing edgy. He turned and walked away while everything within him pleaded to remain.

"Well" she murmured, running her fingers along her lips, "I guess that about says it all, doesn't it, Ricky?" She looked after Justin's departing figure.

Justin went for a walk around the estate, a long one. He needed to cool off.

He needed her, but couldn't accept this reality. The intensity of his feelings overwhelmed him. He wondered if this was what his father had felt each time. If so, what had happened to end it? End it six or was it seven times?

The trouble was, he didn't know what it was that he was doing. She had him so confused, he no longer saw the boundaries of his own life, his own resolve. She had done that to him, that and more. So much more.

She had made him want. At times, she had almost had him believing that it would all work out. Happily ever after.

A cynical smile curled his lips as he rounded a corner and passed Rosalind's well-tended rose garden. Absently, he touched the stem of a rose, its petal pink and soft. Then a thorn jabbed his thumb.

That was it. The beauty of the rose was compelling. It made you forget about what was hidden underneath. The consequences. The pain.

He walked away.

He knew things wouldn't work out with Philadelphia. Hadn't he seen that marriages didn't last? His father, searching for that elusive emotion, had married seven times and found nothing but gold diggers and emptiness. Justin knew that Philadelphia wasn't a gold digger, but a lasting relationship still wouldn't work between them. With all his heart and soul, he wished that it were otherwise. But wishing didn't make it so. Now that he had admitted to it, he had no choice. He had to leave. Walking away now would be considerably less painful than suffering through a relationship that had gone bad.

"I think I feel another cold coming on." Rosalind sniffled dramatically.

Philadelphia turned from the suitcase she was packing under Rosalind's watchful eye and gave the woman a dubious, knowing look. "I don't think so."

Rosalind cleared her throat. "They're my lungs, young woman, not yours. I should know if they're congested."

Philadelphia packed another nightgown, knowing that Rosalind probably wouldn't feel like wearing any of these for at least several days. "It'll be over with before you know it."

Rosalind sat on the side of her bed. "That's what they say about life."

With a snap of her wrist, Philadelphia closed the lid on the Gucci suitcase. "You'll be around to commandeer another whole generation, Rosalind."

She watched as Philadelphia checked the locks to make sure they held. "Think so?"

Satisfied with her effort, Philadelphia turned to look at Rosalind. She smiled affectionately. "I absolutely guarantee it."

Idly, Rosalind ran her finger along the perimeter of the book that was under her hand. "Aries are known to be arrogant."

Philadelphia shook her head. "Confident, Rosalind, confident."

Rosalind laughed, appreciating what Philadelphia was doing. Positive words were good words to hold on to. "Same thing."

"Now there's one of your problems," Justin commented to Philadelphia as he walked into the room. He took Rosalind's hands in his. "A failure of definition."

"I never fail," Philadelphia answered brightly. "I just have setbacks."

"Spoken like a woman who will go far," Rosalind pronounced, eyeing Justin.

"I think she's gone too far already. All set?" he asked Rosalind.

"Yes," Philadelphia answered.

"No," Rosalind announced. But she relented, rising to her feet. Philadelphia was quick to give her her cane; Rosalind had insisted on walking out of the house on her own power. There would be time enough for wheelchairs later. "I suppose there's no putting it off."

"No," Justin said quietly.

Rosalind raised her head high, and leaning on Justin, she proceeded out of the room.

Exits, Philadelphia thought. The lady was very good at exits. As she gathered the necessary items together for Mallory to bring down, Philadelphia fervently hoped that this exit would be a temporary one.

* * *

Philadelphia had never been good at waiting. A restlessness pervaded her entire body. The doctor had warned her and Justin that it was going to be a long operation. He had advised that they go home and return later. The hospital would call them if there was anything urgent. She had stubbornly declined. Philadelphia couldn't have gone home any more than she could have chosen this moment to go off on a carefree vacation. She wanted to be here, wearing a path in the floor, as if her presence would help the operation along somehow.

She glanced at Justin on the sofa. He hadn't moved a muscle since he had sat down. It was, she thought irritably, as if the man was carved out of stone.

"Aren't you tired yet?" Justin asked finally, unable to take her pacing anymore.

She stopped for a moment. "What?"

"You've been pacing around here like a duck at a shooting gallery for almost two hours now." Justin had watched people come and go. That hadn't seemed to deter her. Round and round she went until he had been tempted to grab her and sit on her just to make her stop.

"You've been sitting there like a statue. Don't you have any nerves?" she countered.

He thought of the way she made him feel, of all the desires that had arisen and had to be held in check. "Yes, I have nerves."

She heard the soft edge to his voice, but didn't dwell on it. "Well, where are they?"

"Held in control."

She shoved her hands into the pockets of her jeans and resumed pacing. "Someday you're going to explode."

They were both edgy, he thought. "Probably not until after you wear out."

She sank down next to him with a laugh. "We're quite a pair, aren't we?"

Her hair brushed against his shoulder. He reached out to move it aside, then stopped. Better not to touch anything that belonged to her. "I haven't thought of us that way."

"Yes you have."

This time he did brush her hair away. Firmly. "Do you like to contradict everything I say?"

"Not everything, no." She let out a long breath, then began to rise again. His hand darted out, clamping down on her wrist.

"Sit. The floor could use the rest."

She did, all but melting next to him. "It's going to be all right," she said firmly, whether it was to him or to herself, she wasn't sure.

He took a deep breath. "She's seventy-nine years old."

Philadelphia looked at him, surprised. "Seventy-nine? I thought she said—"

He grinned. He remembered finding an old birth certificate once in his childish exploration of the house. He had never told Rosalind. "She lied."

"Okay, she's seventy-nine. It's still going to be all right."

Where did she get this endless optimism from? "How can you be such a Pollyanna?"

"Maybe I have to be."

He thought of what she had told him about her life, and knew when to back away. "Maybe you do at that."

The operation took another four hours. By then, Philadelphia was ready to climb the walls. Finally, she forced herself to go to the cafeteria for sandwiches, needing to do something in order to keep busy. And she knew that Justin needed to eat. He hadn't had anything since early yesterday evening, unless he snuck down to the kitchen. She doubted that he had. Justin wasn't the type to sneak.

When she returned, the doctor, still dressed in his green operating cap and scrubs, was in the small waiting room, talking to Justin. Her heart began to pound. She nearly dropped the cardboard tray she was carrying.

When the doctor saw her, his worn, leathery face broke into a smile. "She's fine. Came through like the trooper we all knew she was."

Waves of relief washed over Philadelphia. Her tears were evidence of that. "There," she said to Justin, "what did I tell you?" She wiped her cheek with the back of her hand.

"I have no idea," Justin answered, happy enough to be able to tease now that the worst was over. "You talk so much, I can't keep track."

She ignored him. "When can we see her?" she asked Dr. Englund.

"She'll be in her room in an hour," the doctor told them. "I suggest that you two go home after that and get some sleep. You look worse than she does."

"Been giving the man lessons on the art of bestowing compliments, Justin?" Philadelphia asked. The doctor eased out of the room before Justin could answer that.

Philadelphia felt like hugging the world. She started with Justin. Food was forgotten as she suddenly dropped the tray on the flat, marred side table, threw her arms around Justin and kissed him hard.

It was meant as a kiss of relief, as a kiss of joy. The passion was a bonus. It had been lingering on the sidelines, waiting to erupt.

It erupted.

Justin let himself be swept away. He knew that it was going to be for the last time. But he didn't have to tell her that. Not yet.

* * *

The nurse looked up and saw the two of them walk through the automatic doors. "Oh no, you two again," Sheila murmured with a shake of her head. But she was smiling as she said it. "Go ahead, I know there's no use in telling you to take turns. But be quick about it."

"We will," Philadelphia promised. Justin took her hand and pulled her along.

The violet eyes opened for a moment, and Rosalind tried to smile. The tubes running every which way through her body made it difficult to do even that. "Can't be heaven. You two here."

"See, nothing to it," Philadelphia told her, tears gathering in her eyes.

"Said so myself." Rosalind's breathing was labored, but steady. "Here for blessing?"

Justin leaned closer. "What?"

"Shh." Philadelphia gave him a hard poke in the ribs. "Yes."

"Always had them." Rosalind's eyelids slid closed again and she continued to breathe evenly.

"She'll be out for some time," the nurse assured them. They turned to find her standing behind them.

Philadelphia nodded. "Please call us if anything changes. We're going home for a couple of hours." With a renewed spring in her step, Philadelphia led the way out. The automatic doors sprang open, and Justin followed her into the corridor. "Why did you let Aunt Roz think that we were asking her blessings?"

Philadelphia began to walk automatically to the elevators. It seemed like a hundred years ago that they had first entered the hospital. "Did you really intend to argue with a woman who's been anesthetized?" She made it sound ludicrous.

"No."

"She won't even remember it when she comes out. Maybe it'll help her rest peacefully now."

There was an odd smile on Philadelphia's face. He knew it was useless to wonder about it. Better for both of them that he didn't ask.

Chapter Thirteen

The gentle hum of the limousine's engine was the only sound heard on the trip home from the hospital. Mallory kept the glass partition between himself and the passenger section up, having guessed that Justin and Philadelphia wanted their privacy.

Philadelphia could tell from the way Justin sat erect and stiff that he had made up his mind. He had decided to leave. All the signs were there. In the last week, he had mentioned more than once that he would stay until the surgery was over and then he had to get back to work.

Well, the surgery was over.

Visiting Rosalind would present no problem. His office was in Los Angeles, not that far from the hospital. He could visit his aunt every evening after work. And he wouldn't have to run into his aunt's companion, Philadelphia thought. Not if he didn't want to.

Justin turned slightly, casting a glance at Philadelphia. He had never known her to be so quiet; it made him uneasy. He was grateful for the silence, though. If she said anything, if she asked him not to walk out of her life, he wasn't certain that he could. And he knew he had to. For both their sakes.

She wasn't talking. She knew and she understood. It was for the best, he told himself, not for the first time.

The interior of the car was too crowded. All he could smell was the light scent she always wore. He'd never be able to smell wildflowers again without thinking of her.

Justin looked out the window and realized that they were pulling onto the grounds of the estate. A bittersweet sensation passed through him.

The ordeal was over.

He didn't wait for Mallory to come around the side to open his door. Instead, he got out quickly, wanting to have as much distance between him and Philadelphia as he could.

"I'll be taking my own car, Mallory."

Mallory was holding Philadelphia's door open for her, and the older man glanced at her curiously. She merely shrugged. "Very good sir." Mallory's confusion was evident in his voice.

Why was he lingering? Justin wondered. Was he waiting for her to say something? But there wasn't anything to say. He had made up his mind. That used to be enough for him.

"I'm going to my room to pack." It sounded like a nonsensical announcement. Why did he feel compelled to tell her, to say anything at all? He owed Philadelphia no explanations.

"I kind of figured that."

He waited, but no other words followed. No sparring. No witty remarks. No pleas. It obviously made no difference to her if he stayed or left. Why had he thought otherwise?

Because it made a difference to him.

With an annoyed nod of his head, Justin walked quickly into the house and went upstairs.

He packed hurriedly, afraid to stop the momentum once he began. An incredible lethargy threatened to overtake him at any moment. He had no idea why he felt the way he did, why he wanted to hurl the suitcase, clothes and all, against the wall. Why he wanted to stay. With each article of clothing he crumpled into his suitcase—he who always packed so neatly—Justin kept glancing toward the door. It remained shut. He was waiting for it to burst open, followed by a volley of words.

There was no volley, no Philadelphia. Muttering an oath, he finished packing.

Where the hell was she?

Damn it, why was he on edge? This was better, much better. No tears, no entreaties. He had said he didn't believe in relationships, that he knew marriages weren't made in heaven. Hell was more like it. Right? His philosophy, his belief.

She could have at least come to stay goodbye.

When he saw her on the bottom step as he came down the stairs, his heart leapt. Annoyed at his own foolishness, he kept his expression grave. Philadelphia rose when he came to the final step.

He was going to set down the suitcase, then decided that he felt better with it in his hand. No delays. If this had to be done, it had to be done quickly.

"Philadelphia?" His throat felt horribly dry.

"Yes?" She raised her eyes innocently to his.

"You're not going to make this easy, are you?"

She spread her hands wide. "I have no idea what you're talking about."

"Yes you do. You're orchestrating this so that I feel guilty about leaving."

She cocked her head to one side. He wanted to kiss her neck. "How am I doing?"

Defeated, he put the suitcase down temporarily, but continued to hold on to his briefcase. If he had something in his hands, he couldn't take her in his arms and kiss her the way he wanted to.

"It'll never work, Philadelphia. I know that. And I care too much for you to see love die."

She said nothing.

Why wasn't she saying anything? Didn't she care? That made it better, right? So why was he angry? "Are you listening?"

"Yes. You said you loved me."

He sighed. He should have known she'd glean what she wanted to out of this. "I said that I was leaving because relationships don't work and I don't want to see what there is between us die."

"So leaving will make it live?"

"You're twisting things again."

"I'm only trying to understand."

The hell she was, he thought.

She looked a lot less upset than he had pictured in his mind when he had envisioned this scene. "I guess you have to do what you feel is right," she said softly.

"Exactly." He paused, waiting for more of a fight. But there wasn't any.

"So do I."

He looked at her and waited, but there was no more coming. What the hell did that mean? But he knew better than to ask. It would only lead her off on another tangent. "All right. Maybe I'll see you at the hospital."

"Maybe," she echoed.

"Well, goodbye."

"'Bye."

He wanted to kiss her. He knew if he did, he'd be lost. So he didn't.

Because there was nothing else to do, he turned around and walked out the door.

As he crossed the threshold, memories made each step difficult. Philadelphia, the way she looked perched on the hospital chair the first time he saw her, a ragamuffin with a swirl of blond hair. Philadelphia laughing as he dropped the flashlight. The way her eyes grew dark and unfocused when he pulled her into his arms in the hallway and kissed her. The gratitude in her eyes when he handed her a newly destroyed Mr. Tiger. The tears that fell freely when they heard that Rosalind was going to be all right.

As he walked to his car, he waited for her voice to call him back. He waited in vain.

As she stood and watched him walk out, closing the door behind him, Philadelphia began to count softly to herself. She was up to fifty-three when the front door flew open. It banged against the wall.

"Someone let all the air out of my tires!" Justin announced.

He watched as she took her time in coming to him, slowly, like a sleek cat. Every movement of her body made his pulse jump like the needle on a seismograph registering his own private earthquake.

"How awful. Need any help in filling them again?" she asked innocently.

He dropped his suitcase and briefcase on the floor. "You did it, didn't you?"

"Me?" She put her hand to her chest with the sort of dramatic flare she had seen Rosalind employ. "Never. Although, you know," she mused, her eyes laughing, "this might be construed as a message from the stars."

He bit the inside of his cheek to keep from laughing. He didn't want to capitulate too quickly. Although he surmised that she already knew. "What sort of stars would let the air out of tires?"

"Shooting stars?" she offered with a grin. She began to walk past him. "I'll go get—"

"Nothing," he said, grabbing hold of her arm and turning her around to face him. "You will go get nothing. *Do* nothing."

As she looked up into his eyes, she saw everything she needed to. Philadelphia let go of the breath she was holding. He was staying. "I'm not sure I know how to do nothing."

"Learn," he instructed. God, what a mistake he had almost made. "Let me do something for you."

"Several things come to mind right off the bat," she said with a soft laugh. She rose up on her toes and locked her fingers around his neck. Someday, she was going to remember to wear heels around him. But being barefoot seemed so right, so natural. Just as being with him did. "You idiot. I love you and I don't need you in my life to *do* anything except *be* in my life." She considered her words. "No, on second thought, I take that back. I need you to hold me and love me."

He slipped his arms around her waist and drew her against him. "I can do that."

"Good." She nodded her approval.

"You know, even if you hadn't let the air out of the tires, I wouldn't have gotten very far."

"And why is that?"

"Because somewhere between the door and the car, I decided that I was tired of playing it safe all the time. For once, I'm going to take a risk."

"It's never a risk when you have a sure thing."

"You?"

"Me."

"You," he said pointedly, "are never a sure thing. You're like the wind, ever changing, and I've gotten to like that. You've destroyed that precious layer of cautiousness I've wrapped around myself. Being so cautious, I realized that I wasn't real." He pulled her even closer, drinking in her softness, the laughter in her eyes. "Love makes you real. I wasn't real until you came into my life. I walked, I talked, I slept, but I wasn't real. You made me real. You made me *feel*. Marry me, Philadelphia." He saw her eyes open wide with surprise. Uncertainty nibbled at him. After laying himself open like this, would she say no? "What do you say, are you game? I need an answer. In twenty-five words or less."

"Yes."

"Just like that?" He laughed.

"Just like that."

"You know," he told her, kissing the top of her head, "you've still got twenty-four more words left."

"Give me a rain check. I'll use them later."

"I'm sure you will, Philadelphia. I'm very sure that you will." He bent to kiss her and then shook his head. "You know, this is crazy. I've only known you a week."

She framed his face with her hands. "You have the rest of our lives to get to know me better."

He grinned. "Aunt Roz said it would probably take that long."

"Oh?"

"The stars told her."

It was her turn to grin. "Naturally." She tilted her head. "Well, are you going to kiss me or what?"

"Kiss you. The 'or what' will come later."

Philadelphia raised her mouth to his. "Make it soon, Justin. Make it soon."

This time, he fully intended to.

*   *   *   *   *

MORE ABOUT
THE CAPRICORN MAN

by Lydia Lee

If you like a nice, steady climb to the top of the highest mountain, then look no farther than our friend the workaholic Capricorn. Ruled by old man Saturn, with the goat as his symbol, the Capricorn man looks middle-aged in youth, young in old age, has time on his side and a steady goal in mind. He has the determination not only to reach the peaks, but maybe even a few far-flung stars! So what if he takes a few years longer than the other signs? His careful preparation will ensure he *stays* on the top once he arrives. And since he's a nice, practical earth sign, you'd better believe he'll always have a little spare change along the way. He's also often got a pocket full of fear where his security is concerned. However, as the Capricorn man matures, some of that is bound to fall away. But get to the top he must.

If you're interested in getting the Capricorn's attention and perhaps traveling with him to the top of his mountain, you'd better know right off that he's not liable to fall in love at first sight—not second or third sight, for that matter. Of course, miracles do happen but things just don't occur overnight with this man. He needs time. So if you can key his rhythm and practice patience with a capital *P*, you'll find this seemingly shy goat opening up to you.

Just when you thought you had him pegged, he'll surprise you with something slightly poetic, and you'll question if your steady, practical Capricorn is really all that conservative. The answer is yes *and* no. Externally he is conservative, reliable, dependable. Ah, but his inner spirit is full of dreams and banked fires—the kind that can make long winter nights *extra* cozy. Unlike more flamboyant types, the goat gets better as he ages; While our late bloomer might have been just a tad awkward in youth, when it comes to romance, he certainly makes up for it as time goes by.

Where are you likely to find this gem? Somewhere in the upper income level or, if not there already, steadily working in that direction. He'll have an eye on the brass ring; usually a position of power, though not necessarily in the limelight. Look for him in business, in banks and in politics. Capricorn men also make fine builders, architects, dentists and osteopaths. In their own modest way, they'll climb the social ladder in the same way they scale the corporate ladder—with persistence but not too much razzle-dazzle. More likely the Capricorn man will be quietly observing everything, including you. Most especially you, if he thinks you have the qualities he needs to help him scale that ladder: polish, sophistication and enough warmth and sparkle to make up for what he feels he lacks.

This brings us to his Achilles' heel—his vulnerable shyness where matters of the heart are involved. He needs, wants and thrives on love and compliments, perhaps more than the other signs, but it's one of those well-kept secrets that, like everything else to do with Capricorn, will take time to surface. But if you have patience and can slowly draw him out with your special sparkle, his heart *will* open, and stay open for a very long time.

* * * * *

Famous Capricorn Men

George Burns
Humphrey Bogart
Cary Grant
John Denver
Robert E. Lee

WRITTEN IN THE STARS

**Star-crossed lovers?
Or a match made in heaven?**

Why are some heroes strong and silent... and others charming and cheerful? The answer is WRITTEN IN THE STARS!

Coming each month in 1991, Silhouette Romance presents you with a special love story written by one of your favorite authors—highlighting the hero's astrological sign! From January's sensible Capricorn to December's disarming Sagittarius, you'll meet a dozen dazzling and distinct heroes.

Twelve heavenly heroes... twelve wonderful Silhouette Romances destined to delight you. Look for one WRITTEN IN THE STARS title every month throughout 1991—only from Silhouette Romance.

STAR

Silhouette Books®

proudly presents
the long-awaited "prequel" volume of

★ LOVE AND GLORY ★

by
LINDSAY McKENNA

Dawn of Valor

In the summer of '89, Silhouette Special Edition premiered three novels celebrating America's men and women in uniform: LOVE AND GLORY, by bestselling author Lindsay McKenna. Featured were the proud Trayherns, a military family as bold and patriotic as the American flag—three siblings valiantly battling the threat of dishonor, determined to triumph . . . in love and glory.

Now, discover the roots of the Trayhern brand of courage, as parents Chase and Rachel relive their earliest heartstopping experiences of survival and indomitable love, in

Dawn of Valor, Silhouette Special Edition #649.

This February, experience the thrill of LOVE AND GLORY—from the very beginning!

DV-1

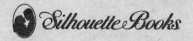

Silhouette Books

You'll flip . . . your pages won't!
Read paperbacks *hands-free* with

Book Mate · I

The perfect "mate" for all your romance paperbacks

Traveling • Vacationing • At Work • In Bed • Studying • Cooking • Eating

Perfect size for all standard paperbacks, this wonderful invention makes reading a pure pleasure! Ingenious design holds paperback books OPEN and FLAT so even wind can't ruffle pages— leaves your hands free to do other things. Reinforced, wipe-clean vinyl-covered holder flexes to let you turn pages without undoing the strap . . . supports paperbacks so well, they have the strength of hardcovers!

Pages turn WITHOUT opening the strap

SEE-THROUGH STRAP

Reinforced back stays flat

Built in bookmark

BOOK MARK

BACK COVER HOLDING STRIP

10 x 7¼ opened
Snaps closed for easy carrying, too

Available now. Send your name, address, and zip code, along with a check or money order for just $5.95 + .75¢ for delivery (for a total of $6.70) payable to Reader Service to:

> Reader Service
> Bookmate Offer
> 3010 Walden Avenue
> P.O. Box 1396
> Buffalo, N.Y. 14269-1396

Offer not available in Canada
*New York residents add appropriate sales tax.

BM-GR

SILHOUETTE·INTIMATE·MOMENTS

NORA ROBERTS
Night Shadow

People all over the city of Urbana were asking, Who was that masked man?

Assistant district attorney Deborah O'Roarke was the first to learn his secret identity . . . and her life would never be the same.

The stories of the lives and loves of the O'Roarke sisters began in January 1991 with NIGHT SHIFT, Silhouette Intimate Moments #365. And if you want to know more about Deborah and the man behind the mask, look for NIGHT SHADOW, Silhouette Intimate Moments #373, available in March at your favorite retail outlet.

NITE-1

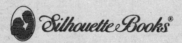